EGG MAN

'Hello.'

The breathing grew louder. 'Is . . . . Is that the painter?' rasped out a voice.

A rush of sweat bubbled out through Brett's bare skin.

'Hello?'

'Hello,' he stammered.

'Is that the painter?'

'Yes.'

The voice wheezed on. Brett's stomach filled with air. Every now and then his voice erupted in a hiccup. When he put down the phone, Mam swam into view like a cardboard cut-out. Her eyebrows rose.

'Who was that?'

'Nelly the elephant,' croaked Brett.

'Oh my God!' gasped Mam. 'You've done it now!'

The EGG MAN

Siân Lewis

RED FOX

A Red Fox Book

Published by Random House Children's Books
20 Vauxhall Bridge Road, London SW1V 2SA

A division of Random House UK Ltd

London Melbourne Sydney Auckland
Johannesburg and agencies throughout
the world

First published by Andersen Press Limited 1992
Red Fox edition 1994

1 3 5 7 9 10 8 6 4 2

Printed and bound in Great Britain by
Cox & Wyman Ltd, Reading, Berkshire

RANDOM HOUSE UK Limited Reg. No. 954009

ISBN 0 09 915000 X

Chapter 1

It was Condor's field that started it.

Looking back it was daft to think you could split with your best friend just because of a field of corn. But Brett had fancied the look of it, just like he sometimes fancied the look of gleaming metallic cars, glazed tiles or a stretch of new-laid road without a mark on it.

Condor's field stretched across the valley floor as smooth and shiny as a plastic sea. From the school bus Brett watched a ray of sun surfboard over it on the back of the breeze. It was only when the breeze blew you could tell it was a field of green corn. He was pressing his nose against the window for one last glimpse, when Mark said in his ear:

'Tonight, after school, we'll flatten that corn.'

'What?' gasped Brett.

'We'll flatten it,' Mark said crisply.

Brett opened his mouth to explain to Mark about the field, then changed his mind. He'd never get Mark to understand. Anyway he had a feeling that Mark was only going to flatten Condor's brill field to spite him.

He wouldn't have tried to save Condor's field, though, if it hadn't been for Winffie and Tim. Mark grabbed hold of them as soon as they got off the bus and told them to meet at the playground on the edge of Greenhill estate at half past six.

'Why d'you do that?' asked Brett.

'You've got to have four to flatten the corn,' said Mark looking coolly at Brett from his great height. In the last year he'd shot up like a beanpole and left Brett way behind him. 'Two's not enough.'

Two had always been enough before. Brett's face went as red as if Mark had hit him, though Mark had never done that in the year and a half they'd been friends. He'd never before got Winffie and Tim to side with him against Brett either.

'Twit!' muttered Brett as he watched his friend swing carelessly up the school drive.

'Eh?' came his brother Steve's voice. 'What's the matter with you?'

'Nothing,' snapped Brett. You couldn't explain to Steve about brill fields either. He swung his bag over his shoulder and slunk off after Mark. You needed to be a superior brain to appreciate the beauty of

Condor's field. Winffie didn't have that kind of brain – no way! – neither did Tim, nor Mark, nor Steve either. Now aliens were a different cup of tea. They had to be superior brains or they wouldn't have got to Earth in the first place, and when their UFOs landed in cornfields, they always made neat regular patterns. He'd seen pictures of them. No clutter or mess, just a perfect circle or two stamped in the corn.

Brett stopped so suddenly that Steve bumped into him for a second time.

'For God's sake!'

'Shove off!' Brett broke into a grin. It was as if an alien had beamed down a message to him from above. Once Mark got an idea into his head, you could never put a stop to it completely, but you could sometimes tinker with it. With luck perhaps he could get Mark to make a UFO pattern in the corn.

He was still trying to explain the pattern to Mark, when they got to the playground at half past six.

'We've got to do it properly,' he muttered, watching Winffie slalom on his bike round the swings. 'There's no point trampling the field any old how.'

'Why not?' Winffie had bionic ears. He veered towards them, bringing his round flat face up close to Brett's.

'It'll just look a mess,' said Brett.

Beside him Mark laughed. He had a glint in his eye and the long loping look of a bendy toy.

'It'll look as if animals done it,' Brett persisted.

Mark laughed again.

'We could do a diamond,' Brett said. One glance at Winffie's face and he knew that the alien circles and whorls he'd seen in photographs in the newspaper were far too ambitious. The diamond was a last resort. He made its shape with his thumbs and forefingers.

'We'll start at the middle of the front of the cornfield,' he said breathlessly. 'Then two of us will cut across this way, two of us will cut across that way till we get to the middle of the sides. Then we'll cut back again and meet up opposite where we came in. Right?'

Mark was still grinning. Winffie was trying to plaster a floppy lock of hair back onto his head. Only Tim looked as if he were thinking.

Brett crouched down and drew a diagram in the dust at their feet.

'So we'll have a diamond with little thingies at each corner,' he cried. 'Right?'

He jumped up so suddenly, his head would have cracked Winffie's chin if Winffie hadn't swayed out of his way in time.

'Hey!' grunted Winffie. He rolled off his bike and let it drop on the ground by the fence.

Mark chuckled. 'Let's go,' he said, getting hold of Brett's shoulder and steering him towards the hedge at the road end of the playground. Brett wriggled free and pushed himself through the thin bit. He was smaller than the others and it was easy for him to get through. He set off down the road without them so as to get to Condor's gate first.

He'd just gone past Nelly the elephant's house when Winffie's piggy squeal reached his ears. He looked back. Mark was at Nelly's gate with his elbow in the air like a shot putter. His other hand punched forward and let fly towards the dark window.

'She's standing behind the curtains, you goop!' squealed Winffie. He grabbed hold of Mark's T-shirt and hustled him along the road at top speed. 'She's at the window!'

'So?' said Mark.

Brett snorted in annoyance. Nelly the elephant was always at the window of her horrible grey house. She was always lurking and peeping at the village kids. It was nothing for Winffie to get worked up about.

'Come on!' he said.

Behind him Mark was explaining to Winffie.

'I didn't throw anything,' he laughed.

'She was AT THE WINDOW!' roared Winffie through his teeth.

'Yeah, but I didn't do anything, did I?' smirked Mark. 'I didn't throw anything. I just pretended. She couldn't touch me.'

Brett ran on to Condor's gate, dodging onto the grass verge whenever the cars came by. The sun had slid behind a veil of thin white cloud and Condor's field lay still, oozing up like glossy paint between the hedges. The others crowded in on him.

'Okay,' said Mark. 'Let's hit it.'

Brett's arm shot out. 'We start at the middle . . . '

'Yeah, yeah!'

They were already scrambling over the gate. Brett plummeted after them down the hill.

'Winffie! Tim! You go over there!' he yelled. 'MARK!'

They were travelling too fast. They'd go crashing straight into the corn.

'MARK!'

Mark braked on the flat at the foot of the hill.

'Shut up, you twit!' he gasped, glancing back at the smooth windows of Condor's Farm up on the main road.

'Winffie!' Brett grabbed him. Winffie pulled loose, shook his head till his hair fell over his eyes and charged. The bottom half of him disappeared. The top half glided over the corn. Tim followed in a cloud of pollen and tiny flies.

Mark had gone too, heading westwards. They were making the diamond! Brett plunged after Mark, widening his path through the stinging, choking corn. At the side of the field Mark swung round. Brett swung too. Winffie and Tim were running towards them at an angle. Deep sappy green lines sliced through the corn and raced towards each other. They were converging like tumbling dominoes, when abruptly Winffie veered to his right. A roar swept after him across the valley from the yard of Condor's Farm.

'HEY!'

Tim wobbled, but kept on course. Mark's long legs had already carried him out of the corn at the point of the diamond. He was diving through the hedge in the direction of the riverbank.

An engine burst into life.

'Condor's got the land-rover out after us!' hiccuped Tim. He skidded round and pounded after Winffie along the hedge.

The stump of a tree helped Brett launch himself into the river field where cows fled, whipping their tails. He always followed Mark, but this time Ray Condor was following too, his land-rover blowing and roaring at the top gate. Down the parallel field it came, smoking and snarling. It was trying to get to the riverbank to cut him off.

Mark had disappeared. Brett tore his way through the clawing hedge, stumbled onto the bank. The grass gave way beneath his feet and sent him crashing into a dry ditch.

'Lie still!' hissed Mark's voice. His foot stabbed Brett's shoulder.

Brett pulled a canopy of grass over the ditch just as the land-rover stopped at the gate. Seconds later it roared onto the riverbank, its shadow skating over their heads. Pollen coated Brett's throat. Each time he breathed, his chest filled the ditch from side to side. Each time he tried to roll over to get his breath, Mark's foot dug into the hollow at the nape of his neck.

As soon as the land-rover was safely past, Brett slid away from Mark and sat bolt upright before he choked to death. Winffie and Tim were scrambling up the rough patch behind Greenhill estate. The land-rover had them in its sights. It was growling up the lane, keeping pace with them. Once they got up to the top, it would nip round to the estate and catch them. That was unless Winffie and Tim made a run for it across the lane to the village.

Brett crawled wheezing out of the ditch. Some horrible squashy thing was sticking to his elbow. He rolled down the bank into the river and scraped his elbow along the stones till the horrible squashy thing went away. He crawled on all fours across the shallow river and wormed his way into a clump of trees on the far bank.

From there he saw Winffie and Tim make their escape across the lane whilst the land-rover sniffed round the houses. With a jerk and a snarl it gave up and came hurtling angrily down the hill and along the riverbank, so close he could see the lines on Ray Condor's face like patterns in the corn. The vibrations rumbled up through the trunks of the trees. As soon as it turned in through the field gate, Mark got up from the ditch and strolled casually back towards home.

For once Brett didn't follow. Instead he crawled up the branches of a spindly tree. Halfway up, he wedged his arm round the lichen-spotted branches and looked down at the pattern in the corn.

It wasn't straight enough for a diamond. It made a tidy eye, though, with a stalk where Winffie'd got scared and run. A sea-green eye. He'd done it! It had worked. No one could deny he'd made his very own pattern and saved Condor's field. When the breeze skimmed over the eye, it winked at him.

Chapter 2

'Brett Jones!'

'Sir?'

'Mark Bates.'

Brett nudged Mark, who was trying to harpoon Nicola Morris's trainers from her bag with his compass. Mark lashed back with his foot.

'MARK BATES!' boomed Cannon Harris, their form teacher.

'Sir?' Mark shot up.

Cannon Harris beckoned. It was his voice that had earned him his nickname. He didn't look so much like a cannon as a statue carved out of granite with eyes deep set beneath a massive overhanging forehead. Before Brett had reached his desk, he'd got up. One heavy hand descended on Brett's shoulder, the other on Mark's. His fingers ground their way into the flesh.

'The rest of you 7B, off you go to your lessons,' the Cannon said hollowly.

Brett turned himself into a rubber tyre. He always did it when trouble was looming. Hard, strong, yet pliable, he stood there ready to absorb whatever Cannon threw at him. It was usually some crap about forgetting homework or mucking about in class. Cannon wasn't that old, but he liked to pretend he was everyone's father.

The rest of the class gurgled out like bathwater. Cannon was trying the silence trick. He stood with sealed lips, his hands getting heavier on their shoulders by the second.

'If only you two spent as much energy on your school work as you do being silly asses,' he ground out at last. 'When are you going to grow up, eh?'

Brett caught Mark's eye. He nearly forgot he was a rubber tyre, nearly let his face crack in a grin. After all there were two of them and only one of Cannon.

'It's not as if you're dull. You just *act* dull, both of you. Two silly idiots together.'

The hands were withdrawn. Cannon's next words hit Brett in the stomach.

'The Headmaster wants to see you in his office.'

'Why?' said Mark sharply.

'Why?' exploded the Cannon. 'Because you two idiots think it's fun to go ruining other people's property, that's why. Off you go.'

Brett quickly straightened his shoulders like Mark,

who was standing his ground and facing Cannon with a furious look in his eye.

'MOVE!' roared Cannon.

Year 8, who were milling at the door, fell away as Mark stalked out, followed by Brett. Cannon drove them down the stairs and along the corridors towards the Headmaster's office on invisible leads. He pinned them both to the wall, leaned over and rapped at the door.

Brett was the first in. The sun made a path across the sea-green carpet towards him and, with a jolt, his mind stopped being rubbery. This wasn't about school. It was about Condor's field.

'Brett Jones and Mark Bates,' said the Headmaster, turning from his filing cabinet with a sarcastic smile on his face. When he was angry, you could see the fizzings in his eyes. Brett had never seen them this close before. Someone knocked at the door behind him and in shuffled Winffie and Tim.

'Wynford Foster and Timothy Beynon,' intoned Cannon.

The Head eyed each boy in turn with eyes like skewers. Brett felt himself punctured on all sides. He had to squeeze his arms against his ribs to stop the air escaping, but Mark stood ramrod straight, almost as tall as the Headmaster.

'Some people work,' ground the Head, easing his way carefully into top gear. 'They drive buses, they build houses, they plant crops! And some people – empty-headed people who don't know what work is –

think they can destroy what others do. They throw bricks, smash windows. They trample down fields of corn! Because they have no imagination, they childishly, mindlessly, trample down the crops that other people have taken hours . . . days . . . weeks to tend. DON'T THEY?'

His face came rushing towards Brett.

'No!' Brett protested.

'No?' The Head puffed himself up, turned white round the nostrils.

Brett gasped. Air was oozing out through millions of tiny holes all over him. He hadn't meant 'No, he hadn't done it.' He meant 'No, it hadn't been mindless.' It had been a diamond, which was much better than just trampling any old how. But he couldn't explain that to the Head. It would never come out right.

'Yes,' he said.

'Yes, Brett Jones,' snapped the Headmaster. 'Yes, yes, YES! You four – all four of you – have been positively identified and named. All four of you were seen last night running through the corn on Mr Condor's farm in St. Hermon!'

Brett flinched. It was only the sun jumping out from behind clouds and shining full in his face, but Cannon thought he was fainting or something. His hand came from nowhere and pinned Brett back into place.

'Now if you can't understand how much trouble and worry you're causing to other people, you'll have to be shown,' said the Headmaster, slamming the cabinet drawer shut. 'Mr Harris is going to find a job that'll take up your dinner hours for the rest of this week. It's time you found out what work is.' He paused icy-eyed and nodded at the Cannon. 'Right, off you go. And any more nonsense and your parents will be called to see me. Understand?'

Brett glanced at Mark. Mark didn't move a muscle. Mark's dad would go berserk if he knew. That was why Condor had complained to the school and not to their homes. Someone must have told him to do that.

'Wynford!' Cannon was clearing his throat. 'Open the door. Out you all go and wait for me in the staffroom.'

In the staffroom where the chairs were at odd angles as if talking to each other, they stood just inside the door. Winffie kept jerking his head and slapping his hair back.

'Who did it?' said Mark through his teeth.

'What?' croaked Brett.

'Grassed on us?'

'Condor?'

Mark shook his head. 'Condor doesn't know us. He's hardly been in St. Hermon a year.'

The Head's door closed softly and Cannon came padding into the room. Even his voice had come down ten decibels.

'Boys,' he said sadly. 'You brought all this on yourselves, you know.'

Mark sniffed. Cannon couldn't tell whether it was a rude sniff or an ordinary sniff, but his voice hardened.

'You make sure you bring some old clothes tomorrow,' he rapped out. 'You're going to paint the animal shed each dinner hour, till you've finished. And I want it done properly. No messing around.' He was staring at Mark and Mark was staring back straight in his eyes. Cannon gave up first. 'Understand, Brett?' he said.

''s, sir.'

'Wynford? Timothy? Mark?'

Mark didn't want to understand. His brain was short-circuiting. Brett could see the sparks behind his eyes. As Cannon hustled them down the corridor, he spoke from the corner of his mouth:

'It was Nelly the elephant.'

'Wha . . . ?'

'She told Condor.'

Mark ground his knuckles hard against the palm of his hand, but you couldn't crush an elephant that easy.

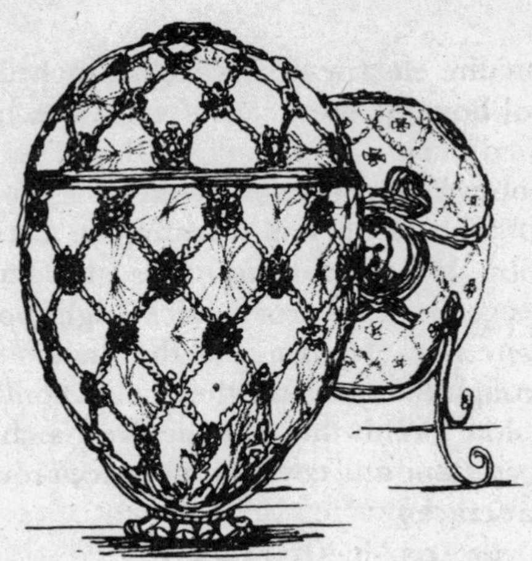

Chapter 3

You could crush her broad beans, though.

'Tomorrow,' Mark hissed. 'And the day after and the day after that. That's three days we'll be losing our dinner hour, bet you. We'll get three of her beans for that.'

He and Brett were standing in the lumpy field behind Nelly the elephant's garden, just the two of them. The garden was lumpy too, except for the square patch in the middle that Ted Morgan from the village had planted with onions, potatoes and beans. The beans were in flower, marching in a long straight row along the edge of the patch.

The patch lay halfway between the straggly hedge and the dark window of the elephant's kitchen. Mark pulled a pair of pliers from his pocket and cut three lengths of the electrical wire he'd pinched from his dad's tool-box. At the head of each one he made a noose.

'Got your stone?' he asked Brett.

'Yeah.' The stone was warming in Brett's hand, egg-shaped. He opened and closed his fingers. The stone was getting so warm a chick might pop out of it any minute now. He dragged the fingers of his free hand through the grass till they made contact with a piece of shale. With the shale he drew a chick on the egg-shaped stone and covered the space around it with triangular cracks.

'Get a move on,' hissed Mark.

It was almost a pity to get rid of the egg-shaped stone, but he couldn't find another big enough as he crept along Nelly the elephant's side hedge. By the time he'd reached the front garden wall Mark was already signalling. Brett got to his feet and let fly with the stone.

The stone nearly whizzed out through the wrought-iron gate. A curly leaf-pattern fielded it just in time and batted it back up Nelly the elephant's path. It crashed against her front doorstep and bounced all the way down along the path with a heck of a noise. Brett went haring up towards Mark. Behind him Nelly the elephant's front door was opening. She was always lurking behind her dingy curtains waiting for things to happen.

'Hurry!' he gasped, but Mark was already through the hedge, the electrical wires trailing behind him.

Brett grabbed the ends. Through the privet branches he saw Mark lasso the three tallest broad beans, tug the nooses tight round their stalks and come racing back.

He beat Nelly the elephant easily. Usually she opened the front door, checked there was no one in the front garden, then came rumbling like a tank to the back. Mark was safe behind the hedge long before the bolts squealed and Nelly filled the doorway in her massive tent of a dress. Her head was sunk into her shoulders like a plum set on top of a mouldy bun. The plum swivelled.

'Pull!' Mark hissed.

At one and the same time three broad bean plants hopped out of the soil of Nelly the elephant's garden and fell flat on their backs.

Nelly the elephant gave a grunt like a pig. Brett giggled out loud.

'Boys!' bellowed the elephant in her deep voice. 'Boys!'

'Pull!' spluttered Mark.

The three broad bean plants wriggled and hopped over the lumpy ground, then nosedived into the hedge. Nelly the elephant came trundling in pursuit. They waited till she was almost on top of them before creeping down the side hedge. After he'd rolled over the gate onto the pavement, Brett looked back and saw Nelly wrenching a broad bean plant from the hedge with her big behind in the air. She turned round just in time to catch a glimpse of two backs disappearing down the main road.

Mam's Metro beeped behind them. Brett plunged through the hedge, cut across the children's playground and stood on the corner hitching a lift. Mam pulled a face and drove on.

'Mean!' he called, chasing her round the corner.

Mam waved from the far end of the street. Mark's dad was out pushing their clapped-out mower across the front lawn. The wrinkles above his nose were deep enough to hold two slices of toast.

Mark pushed the electrical wire right down inside the pocket of his jeans.

'I think I'll forget to take my old clothes to school tomorrow,' he said.

'Why?' said Brett.

'Cannon can't make me paint in my school clothes or my dad will pulverise him,' said Mark.

'Yeah,' said Brett.

'You taking yours?'

'We can't both of us forget,' muttered Brett.

'Twit!' The remark was aimed both at Brett and at Ainsleigh, next door. Ainsleigh was out in his boiler suit painting the twirly bit of fencing round his mini-fishpond. Ainsleigh was a painter. That was his job. But it took him three hours just to paint a door, Brett's mam said. That's why she wouldn't have him. He was too expensive.

Ainsleigh dabbed yellow paint on a loop of fence, then leaned over sideways with his ear on the lawn and squinted up to see if it was painted underneath.

'The worms have got to tell him what to do,' muttered Mark. 'He's just one big fat worm himself.'

Brett burst into a giggle. Ainsleigh looked round and his big horse teeth grinned at them.

'How are you then, boys?' he said.

'Okay,' said Mark.

'So you bloody should be!' yelled his father over the noise of the mower. 'Come on. Give us a hand with this.'

Fast as Mark moved, the mower let out a whirring screech and stopped dead before he got to it.

'Time these boys learnt to do something,' Len Bates grunted in Ainsleigh's direction. He slammed the mower handle into his son's hand.

Ainsleigh said nothing. His face remained locked in a grin. Brett edged towards him. Seeing Mark's dad in a mood made him feel glad his own dad had left home ages ago and was living in town.

'I'm going to do some painting tomorrow,' he whispered to Ainsleigh, so that they could shut out Mark and his dad.

'Are you?' Ainsleigh shifted his eyes from next door. It took ages for him just to look surprised. His forehead creased at the rate of a slow-motion replay. 'Good lad!' he cried at long last. 'What are you painting?'

'The animal shed in school where they keep pet gerbils and things.'

Ainsleigh, of course, thought he was doing it from the kindness of his heart.

'Good lad!' he cheered, giving Brett a pleased shake with his paint-free hand.

Brett glanced round to see if Mark had noticed, but Mark was struggling with the starting handle of the mower. The mower was playing a game with him, pretending to start and then choking. Pull...growl... pull. Mark jerked like a puppet, whilst his dad's fleshy face got pucer and pucer.

'Get out of my WAY!'

Len Bates elbowed Mark aside fiercely and wrenched at the mower's starter. On the third pull the mower roared and went on roaring till the choke was pushed in. As soon as it settled into a hiccupy rumble, Mark took his dad's place and pushed the mower gingerly across the lawn. Brett and Ainsleigh chatted and tried to pretend they weren't listening, but each time the mower coughed, they both went quiet. Then when Len Bates went back into his house at last, Ainsleigh scratched his head as if he were trying to get rid of something from his curly hair.

Apart from his freckles Ainsleigh had an interesting pattern of spots nestling among the blond hairs on his arm, the tiniest of spots, mostly white with a dash of yellow and blue and one spot of green. His hands were pink and scrubbed and smelled of white spirit. At the touch of those hands the green twisty fence turned a startling yellow. Brett looked up at the house. The window frames were bright yellow too.

'When did you paint them?' he asked.

'Last week,' Ainsleigh chuckled. 'You hadn't

noticed, had you? Bet you will from now on. Now you're a painter you'll start getting a painter's eye like me. I always notice when things have been painted.' He put his ear to the ground again to check the underneath of a loop. 'I've got some left-over paints I can give you, if you want to do some painting,' he said.

Mark's mower choked. It could have been Mark himself choking. He'd laugh himself sick if he thought Brett was going to turn into a second Ainsleigh. Brett glanced round slyly, but Mark was too busy struggling with the machine. He still had one narrow strip of lawn left. His dad's face appeared in the window and Mark's arm jerked back in a shock that set the mower roaring again.

'Okay?' said Ainsleigh.

'Yeah,' said Brett.

His eyes slid across from Ainsleigh's house to Mark's. Mark's window-sills were flaking. He caught Len Bates's eye and turned his head away.

'Thanks,' he said to Ainsleigh and scrambled to his feet.

'Any time...' Ainsleigh shifted round. He'd have gone on repeating offers of help, if Brett hadn't made his escape. He'd seen Mam out the front looking for him. As he raced down the road, she disappeared back into the house.

'Mam!' He collided with the front door and slithered down against the rising tide of chipped paint. 'Yuck!' he cried as his mam opened up. 'This door's gone disgusting!'

'Oh yeah?' said Mam with a sly grin. 'It's been like that for ages. How come you noticed now?'

Brett flushed and checked in the mirror in case he'd suddenly grown big horse teeth.

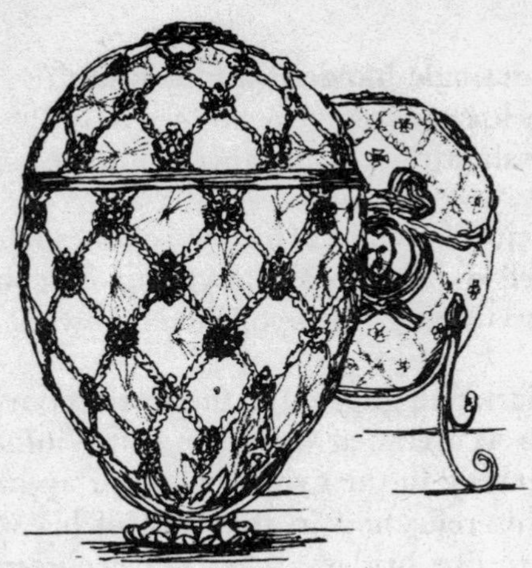

Chapter 4

He kept his mouth shut on the bus in case Mark noticed. He kept his mouth shut all morning. He couldn't let on to Mark that he fancied doing a bit of painting. Ever since the night before there'd been an itch in his fingertips that he couldn't ignore.

Mark was in one of his twitchy loud moods. His face was dead white beneath his jet-black hair and a blue vein throbbed on the side of his temple. Mark always got extra-loud whenever he was copping it and this time Cannon had nearly gone through the roof.

'Mark Bates!' he roared. 'You're the sort of fellow who'd deliberately put his foot in a trap. Well, traps close, Mark. Traps close. Since you can't paint without your old clothes, you'll report to me at twelve-fifteen prompt in the store-room. You'll have to tidy the shelves single-handed. Understand?'

Mark's lips moved.

'Understand?'

'Sir.'

Brett felt the weight of his own clothes lying against his foot. He didn't dare say anything. He couldn't. For once he was letting Mark cop it on his own.

When Mark had gone off to the store-room at twelve-fifteen, Brett breathed again. He and Winffie and Tim were changing in the gym. He curled up his lips and studied his reflection in the back of his watch. His teeth were like bridge arches. They weren't horse's teeth at all.

While he was admiring himself, Winffie went sniffing out through the door with Tim behind him.

'Hang on!' Brett cried.

He leapt after them down the bank. Cannon was already at the shed with a large tin of paint and a bowl at his feet. Brett pretended he couldn't stop and got to him first, just as he was levering the lid off the paint tin.

'Yuck!' gasped Brett when he saw what was inside.

'What's wrong, Jones?' Cannon growled.

'Paint's gone off, sir!' said Brett dropping down beside him in dismay. The paint was all stuck together like semolina pudding. It didn't look a bit like Ainsleigh's lovely bright shiny stuff.

'It's jelly paint, daft,' sniffed Winffie stubbing his toe on the tin. 'It says so, don't it?'

'And it's undercoat,' said Cannon, straightening quickly and taking the tin with him. Brett followed it like a hungry dog. 'You'll be covering it with green tomorrow. So for today I'd like you to work fast. Don't leave any lumps. Cover all the wood, but don't worry if it looks patchy. And be careful with the paint. Try not to spill it on yourselves.'

Cannon produced three brand new paint brushes from his pocket, ignored Winffie's outstretched hand and gave Brett first pick. Brett tested the soft bristles on the palm of his hand. He watched impatiently as Cannon splodged paint into the bowl that turned out to be three margarine pots one on top of the other. As soon as the first pot was full, Brett squatted over it and let his paintbrush slide over the edge and just rest on the jelly.

'Now you're one person short,' began Cannon, 'so...'

'I'll do it,' said Brett without thinking. A dribble fell onto the knee of his jeans.

Cannon chuckled. 'You can help each other,' he said. 'Just work fast so we can get it all finished this week. See how you get on.'

Brett eased the brush into the jelly paint and watched the globules of white spring onto the bristle tips. Cannon's breath ruffled his hair.

'Wipe the excess on the side of the bowl,' Cannon said.

Brett wanted Cannon to go away so he could just see what it felt like to touch the shed with his brush. Winffie was already slapping paint on the door with his mouth open to catch the drips. Gingerly Brett stood up and made feathery dabs on the top corner of his side. He watched the wood drink in the paint. Cannon did too. Once Cannon had gone, Brett drew his brush right along the wall of the shed.

Winffie was snorting and in the gloom inside the shed a gerbil was testing its wheel. Brett felt as though it were Christmas morning. He felt bubbles coursing up and down his veins. It was scary. The bubbles rushed out through his brush. He tried painting a triangle and filling it in with a coating of paint as thin and shiny as a fly's wing. Then Winffie poked his nose round the corner and made the triangle go smudgy.

'Need more paint,' Winffie sniffed.

'Not already!' gasped Brett.

Round the side of the shed sauntered Tim with his paint bowl.

'I've nearly finished,' he said casting a critical eye over Brett's unpainted side.

'So?' said Brett crossly.

'I'll start on Mark's side when I've finished. You'll be here all day, you will.'

Brett grunted. He wished Winffie and Tim miles away. The thought of them made his arm ache. He flexed it, just as Mark sometimes flexed his arm when his dad had punched him one. Winffie swept round him, bowl in hand, and Tim joined him at Mark's end of the shed. He could hear their old brushes slap against the wood.

Brett still had half his paint left, but he went to pour

himself some more just so he could sneak a look at Winffie's painting. Ha! He almost snorted out loud when he saw it. It was just iike Winffie himself. Slobby. Winffie might know about paint, but he didn't know *how* to paint at all. His own side looked miles better.

And for once his eyes weren't playing tricks on him. When Cannon came back, he said, 'Good work, Brett,' in a surprised voice, which he didn't to the others.

Brett couldn't help giving Cannon a smug grin. He'd covered the grin by the time he got into class, but he'd forgotten to scrub out the shine in his eyes and Mark saw it.

Chapter 5

Mark's thin sharp face hung broodingly over Brett when they got off the school bus. He didn't like it when Brett tried something different. His face was so sharp it made Brett want to wriggle his shoulders. He was quite glad when they got to Mark's house and he could run off down the road to catch up with his brother Steve. Steve, though, ran faster and shut the front door in his face.

'Swine!' yelled Brett.

By the time he'd managed to fish out his key and run upstairs, Steve was already struggling into his jeans in the bedroom they shared. His shoes lay stinking in the middle of the floor. Brett kicked them under the bed.

'Temper temper!' Steve said cheerfully.

'You've crossed the border,' Brett snapped. He

marched across the floor and marked out the imaginary line that stretched from the middle of the window to a point above the left-hand knob of the chest-of-drawers. Steve had to keep his posters and junk on the far side of the line, Mam had said, but Brett still had to look at his brother's mess or go round with his eyes closed. 'You're a pig,' he said.

'And you're my brother,' grinned Steve.

'Once Darren gets a flat in town, you can move into his room,' said Brett.

'That'll be in about ten years' time.'

Steve stumbled over his school bag and hopped downstairs, pulling his trainers on at the same time. Brett watched him get his bike and fishing rod from the garage. Steve was the filthiest pig in the world. It wasn't fair! Other people didn't have to share rooms. When he opened the window to yell after him, bits of putty dropped off the frame and trickled onto the path below.

Brett felt all itchy with annoyance. His room was a dump. His house was a dump – and just to show how much of a dump it was, the sun skipped down the road and polished up the Evanses' front door opposite. Ainsleigh had painted it such a shiny tingly toothpasty green, it made you want to take a bite out of it. Brett heard his mother's car turn into the street and went downstairs to grumble to her.

'Mam.'

His mother's legs came out of the car first, followed by the squirming rest of her.

'Grab hold of the bag, Brett,' she puffed.

The shopping bag tumbled over her shoulder and bounced off the steering wheel where Brett grabbed it. Mam gave her shoulderbag a fierce jerk and edged out backwards, bumping Brett out of the way.

'Whatzzatyougotonyourfinger?' The words came streaking out like a high speed train, before she'd had time to pull her blouse down.

'What?' Brett peeped round the bag. Mam had seen the blob of paint on the inside of his middle finger. Trust Mam! He hadn't washed it off, because that bit of finger was sore after holding the paintbrush. 'Paint.'

'What've you been up to now? You boys, honestly! I've had it up to here. I've been working all day...'

'I've been painting the animal shed in school.'

'Eh?'

'Cannon told me to.'

'Oh!' His mam had puffed herself up like a magic beanstalk. She was wearing her highest-heeled sandals. Suddenly she puffed herself down again. It was easier to believe him than not to. She pulled her blouse beneath the armpits to let the heat out. 'I thought you and that Mark... Oh well, never mind.' She put her arm round his shoulder to make amends.

Once inside the house she kicked off her sandals so as to bring herself down a bit closer to his level and laughed.

'Come on,' she said. 'Let's you and I have a sneaky cup of tea before the others come in.'

'Any strawberries?' He pushed his nose into

her bag.

'Clubs,' she said, plugging the kettle in. 'The strawberries were mouldy by the time I got to the shop. Got 'em?'

'Yeah.'

Brett sat at the kitchen table and hooked his legs round the stool. He waited for his mam to throw the teabag into the pot. She only boiled up enough water for a quick cupful each. Then she lit up her only cigarette of the day.

'What's the matter with you?' she asked through the smoke.

'Nothing.'

'Brett Jones!' She poked his shoulder. 'You can't fool me.'

He grinned. He'd had an idea, but he wasn't going to say a word till her hands were curled round that cup of tea and she was melting over it. It was her best time of day.

Only she didn't melt. She kept on peeping at him from the corner of her eye and making him giggle.

'Mam,' he said at last. 'You know when Darren moves out?'

'Moves out!' Mam snorted. 'How's he going to pay for a room in town? He hardly gets anything in that supermarket.'

'Yeah, but when he does,' persisted Brett, 'can I have my room painted?'

Mam didn't answer. She let a grin spread over her face. She was only thirty-four, his mam, which was quite young compared to Mark's mam.

'Brett Jones,' she began.

'I can do it,' said Brett. 'Cannon said I was good.'

'Well, that's something. You're just like your dad, you are,' chuckled Mam without any bitterness. 'Your dad always had big ideas. It's painting now, is it?'

Brett ignored her. 'I don't have to wait for Darren,' he said. 'I can do it now.'

''Course you can,' his mam rejoined. 'And who's going to pay for the paint and clear up after you?'

'I am,' said Brett to the second part of her question. 'And Ainsleigh's promised to give me paint.'

'Has he indeed?' Mam shook a Club out of its packet and slid it across the table to him. A little ball of ash bounced after it. Mam was nursing her cigarette. She hardly smoked it at all really. She just watched the fire nibble it away.

'Yes,' said Brett. He knew he was putting his foot in it. This was Mam's quiet time and she didn't like to be hassled, but he couldn't stop himself. 'Steve's a filthy pig. You don't have to smell his filthy shoes and look at his spotty old wall!' he burst out.

Mam sighed.

'You don't,' said Brett. 'He...'

'Shut it now, Brett,' Mam said in an ominous voice.

'I can...'

'Shut it!'

'If Ainsleigh gives me the paint,' Brett said, drowning her out, 'will you let me do it?'

'Hell!' spat his mother. The ash had dropped off the

cigarette and spilled onto her skirt. She jumped up. Brett thought she was going to have a go at him and shot out of the back door.

He stopped to cool off in the garage. Once Mam cooled off too, she'd understand. It wasn't a daft plan. He was twelve and all his friends had rooms of their own. None of them had to share with a stinking brother. He poked his head out to see if Ainsleigh was around and instead saw Mark skidding down the road on his bike.

Mark just swung round without a word and rode off slowly enough for Brett to catch up on his own bike. Then off they both went, pedalling like mad through the village and up the hill on the other side till their arms and legs turned to jelly. This was a recipe they sometimes used when they were fed up. Instead of holding up two fingers and getting told off by your mam or punched by your dad, you just pedalled and pedalled till you were too tired to care any more. But the first thing Brett saw, when he collapsed in the hedge, was Condor's field spread out below him on the valley floor and he just had to roll over and part the grass for a better look.

The wind had been at the field since Monday night. It had gone over the corn like a flying elephant, pressing bits and flattening them not quite to the ground. The eye was still there, but the field looked a mess.

'That's not worth three days of stupid slog!'

growled Mark.

Brett said nothing. Mark snorted and let his bike slide off down the hill without any brakes on.

Chapter 6

The next night Mark went down the village on his own. It was the first time he'd gone off to play without telling since he came to live in Robin's house in Greenhill.

Robin had been Brett's best friend. When Mark came to the village school, Mrs Jenkins had put him to sit by Brett at the table in the corner. Mark was as tall as Brett was short and Mark could do things, whereas Brett only had fancy ideas in his head. In the end Mrs Jenkins moved them both to the front to keep an eye on them.

'Why aren't you out with Mark?' Steve asked after supper.

'Haven't got to be.' Brett shrugged.

'Don't tell me the terrible twins have quarrelled.

Mam will be pleased,' crowed Steve from the depths of his duvet where he was lying on his back with one foot in the air pulling his trainer on and scattering dried mud all over his face.

'I'm going to paint this room,' said Brett just to get one back on him.

Steve hooted.

'Ainsleigh's going to give me paint,' said Brett. He'd been keeping watch for Ainsleigh since six o'clock. That was after he'd seen Mark go off down the village without him. Mark had been in a mood after painting the shed at school.

'You're mad,' said Steve, getting up and stretching to show off the twelve centimetres he'd grown in a year. 'Mam will never let you do it. You're bound to make a muck-up. You always do.' He shot over Brett's half of the room and through the door before Brett could fling a stinking shoe after him.

Brett got him as he was going for his bike. He threw a bit of putty on his brother's head. Steve pulled a grinny face as he swung off with his fishing-rod under his arm.

Brett went carefully down to find his other brother, Darren. Darren was the only one with any sense. Since he'd got himself a job and a girlfriend, he sat around the house looking neat and smelling of bath oil. If he made such a big thing of looking tidy himself, he was bound to want the house to look tidy as well. He should understand.

Darren was lounging in front of the business news

on telly, his hair still wet from the shower.

Brett said: 'Steve's the muckiest pig in the world.'

'Yeah,' said Darren.

'You're lucky you haven't got to share a room with him.'

'I used to,' said Darren.

'Well, he's worse now he's bigger.'

'You can't paint a *room*,' said Darren. 'Not a *room*.' Steve must have told him about Condor's field and the animal shed. Neither of them had told Mam or she'd have gone spare. She'd been snappy to Mark ever since he and Brett had set fire to the bracken down by the river over half-term, and that had been an accident. She always blamed Mark for everything, as if he, Brett, didn't have a mind of his own.

'Well, I'm going to,' said Brett.

'Go you,' said Darren amiably. 'You always have big ideas, you do.'

'Since when?'

'Since always,' grinned Darren. 'And you always get fed up with them. Remember when you were going to change the back garden into an adventure playground and make up your own games? You pestered...'

'Yeah, well it wasn't my fault Mam stopped me!' Brett was already snorting out through the door. You couldn't even punch Darren any more. He looked too soft and stupid. Brett slammed the front door, then crept round the corner of the house and sat there waiting.

The trick was to get hold of Ainsleigh when his wife wasn't around. Jean not only had eyes like a hawk, she had a sharp nose to match, ready to blind any boy who got within five metres of Ainsleigh's paint tins. That was mainly because of Mark whose football had caused the blue splodge in the middle of her garage floor.

The thud of a dustbin lid behind Ainsleigh's house brought Brett to his feet. He could tell it was Jean by the way the lid was being neatly screwed back on. If Jean was scraping off the supper plates, it meant she was washing up and Ainsleigh was out pottering. With a quick glance to make sure Mark wasn't back, Brett padded up the street.

Ainsleigh was in his garage nursing a plant pot with a white wooden aeroplane stuck in it. The sun went skidding along the paint tins on the shelves and Ainsleigh's eyes went skidding along after it. He was just reaching up when he saw Brett and his long horsy face broke into a smile.

'Okay, Brett?'

'Yeah.'

Brett paused and let his eyes fix on the aeroplane. Ainsleigh was always dead keen on showing things.

'What d'you think?' Ainsleigh grinned.

'That's a funny flower,' said Brett.

Ainsleigh chuckled. He put the pot down on his work bench and gave the aeroplane's over-large propellers a twirl. Brett went down to examine it. He was allowed a twirl too.

'This is going to go out in the garden so it'll turn in the wind,' Ainsleigh explained.

'Wow!' said Brett. Who'd have guessed?

'But I'm going to paint it first,' said Ainsleigh. 'That's why I've planted it. To hold it steady.'

Ainsleigh winked in slow motion. He was still winking as he opened the cupboard beneath the work bench. From the cupboard he brought out a slim brush, the width of two pencils, with a silver band and turps-smelling bristles which he tested on the back of his hand.

'Yellow,' he said, lifting a tin off the shelf and opening it in front of Brett's nose.

'Oil paint,' said Brett just to show he knew what the brown stuff was on top of the paint. Cannon had shown him when they did the shed.

'Over to you, Mr Jones,' said Ainsleigh, holding the brush out.

Brett looked into Ainsleigh's eyes. A nasty feeling began to niggle his stomach. What if Ainsleigh wasn't going to give him paint after all, but just make him piddle about with a stupid aeroplane?

'Go on,' said Ainsleigh. 'Don't be scared.'

'I'm not scared,' scoffed Brett, taking the brush.

The paint was a long way down at the bottom of the tin like scrambled eggs. He dipped in the bristles, wiped off the extra and gripped the aeroplane by its rod.

The propellers quivered as soon as the brush

touched the plane. He made it come to life like a butterfly emerging from its chrysalis. He'd seen that happen once in school. Ainsleigh watched without a word.

'Ainsleigh!'

He didn't even answer when Jean called.

'Ainsleigh!' She clattered through the back door in her mules.

Ainsleigh's breath escaped at last through his nose. The aeroplane was nearly done. One last brilliant dab on the cockpit and he turned to face Jean proudly.

'I didn't know Brett was a painter.' Jean's voice fell in a fog on the garage. It would have grounded any aeroplane except Brett's. Silently, gracefully, Brett's yellow plane soared, bouncing sunlight off its wings. Ainsleigh held it up high.

'Eeeee-oooow,' he said softly, bringing it back down to earth and grinning at Brett. Brett grinned back. His fingers tightened on the paintbrush. He could have painted a whole squadron of planes, a fleet of Yellow Arrows flashing and zooming beneath the garage roof.

'I didn't know Brett was a painter,' Jean repeated.

'Brett!' came an echoing voice.

Mam was up on the road. One flip-flop slid from under her as she walked down the slope to the garage and she hooked it back with vermilion toes.

'I didn't know Brett was a painter,' Jean said to her.

Mam laughed. She watched Ainsleigh take the brush from Brett's hand. He brought out a cloth and a bottle of white spirit. Brett wiped the back of his hands and his fingers. In the palm of his left hand he left a splash of yellow paint. It was his ejector button. He might need it some day.

Ainsleigh jiggled the aeroplane till its gi-normous propellers spun in front of Mam's nose.

'Like it?' he asked.

'So that's what you painted, Brett?' grinned Mam.

She thought it was funny, after all his boasting about painting a room, but Brett was watching Ainsleigh. Ainsleigh had stepped back and was giving the shelves a critical look.

'I said I'd give you some paint,' he murmured. 'Fair play to the boy. If he likes painting, why not?'

Brett shot a triumphant glance at his mam.

Ainsleigh hooked his finger under the rim of a tin, eased it over the edge of the shelf and caught it. He put it down on the floor and prised off a second tin. Then he moved the tins across with his foot to the work bench. From the cupboard below he selected a brush. The handle had a worn look, but the bristles spread out soft and silky against Ainsleigh's palm.

'Here.' He thrust it at Brett.

Brett's grin stretched from ear to ear.

'And these.' Ainsleigh edged the tins over.

'Thanks.'

The tins were lighter than Brett expected. They couldn't be half-full, but that didn't matter. Jean was backing away as if he were carrying deadly germs.

'You can practise a bit with those,' Ainsleigh called after him.

‘Yeah.’ He stopped at the top of the drive and grinned at Ainsleigh and Jean like a goon. Mam came flopping behind. She put on a spurt to catch up with him and yanked at the tin in his right hand. She gave a funny sort of sniff before letting go. Then she crossed the lawn quickly to the front door.

Brett took his precious tins to the back of the garage where no one could see him. He settled down beside them with a chisel in his hand.

There he opened the tins one after the other – and swore!

Chapter 7

'Bloody Ainsleigh!'

'Brett!' roared Mam.

'What's the matter?' Darren poked his head round the kitchen door.

'He's given me sh...'

'BRETT!'

'...yellow and some horrible pink!'

'Well, did he know you wanted to paint your bedroom?' yelled Mam.

'No.'

'Well, there you are then. You're supposed to paint aeroplanes and things with it. It's only for practice. That's what he said. You can paint...you can paint those planters out the back for me. Anyway you mustn't go round begging at Ainsleigh's. That's why I was calling you.'

'Wasn't begging!' Brett bolted upstairs. Behind him he could hear the murmur of Mam and Darren's voices disintegrate into puffy giggles. He slammed his bedroom door so hard that Steve's poster of Madonna slid sideways and hung by one lump of Blu-tack before giving up the ghost and diving down the side of his bed. Now there were four more filthy hairy blobs of Blu-tack stuck on the wall just in front of his eyes when he turned over in bed. Brett plunged his head under his pillow. Five minutes later when Darren came up, he lashed out with his foot.

'Look,' said Darren. 'You can always advertise for odd jobs.'

'Odd jobs!' Brett got a mouthful of pillow and spat.

'Painting odd jobs.'

Brett snorted. Through a small tunnel beneath the pillow he could see a shiny button on Darren's shirt. Even his buttons shone.

'Gareth Morgan used to.'

Brett sniffed. The pillow reeked of Daz.

'Gareth Morgan used to,' Darren persisted. 'He used to put a notice "Odd Jobs: £2.50 an hour" in the shop window and he got some too.'

'I haven't got any paint,' sniffed Brett rolling over onto his back. 'Except yucky pink and...'

'Yeah, well the people you're working for will buy that. You don't have to buy it.'

Brett lay still, suffocating. He could just imagine his mam saying: 'Yeah, let the kid do a bit of painting.

He'll soon get sick of it.'

'Okay?' said Darren. 'I'll help you with the notice if you like.'

Brett kicked out.

Once Darren had gone back downstairs, he slid out from under the pillow, his face all sweaty. He buried his face in the duvet to dry the sweat off. When he resurfaced, he felt raw as a skinned rabbit. It was like he felt when he first heard that Robin was going away. 'Don't be so daft,' his mam had said. 'You can stand on your own two feet. You're your own man now.' 'MAN!' she said.

Brett felt so fed up he could hardly stand at all. He flopped against the window-sill and pressed his cheek against the warm glass. Down below the sun was polishing up Ainsleigh's spotless white van with the deep blue lettering. He'd seen it so often he knew it off by heart:

Ainsleigh Vaughan
Painter and decorator
Tel: St.Hermon 651

Ainsleigh Vaughan... Brett recited it over and over, but Mam and Darren had already settled in front of Wimbledon on telly by the time he'd plucked up courage to sneak downstairs. From the kitchen he pinched an old Fashion Show invitation card that had been hanging around on the window-sill for ages.

Back in his bedroom again he tried sorting out the notice in his head:

PAINTING
Evenings and weekends
£2 an hour
Apply: Brett Jones, 21 Greenhill, St.Hermon.
Phone: St.Hermon 316

Once he was satisfied, he got a Berol pen from Steve's bag and printed it out. The 6 went extra-squiggly as Mark rang the doorbell.

Mark was in one of his teasing moods. With his long legs he'd streak way ahead on his bike, stop, then streak way ahead again. Whenever Brett caught up, he said: 'Painting's for dull stupid twits like Ainsleigh,' and waited for Brett to agree.

Brett just gasped, out of breath. He couldn't have agreed even if he wanted to and for once he didn't want to. It was like his mam always said. He didn't have to go along with everything Mark said or did, especially now that Mark had gone down the village on his own. Mark raced on again. He got back to Greenhill before Brett and was standing astride his bike when Brett came round the corner. He dropped his bike as soon as he saw Brett and strolled off into the house.

Brett rode his own bike into the garage. His legs were pulsating and the spot on his finger where the paintbrush rubbed was stinging like mad. As soon as he stepped inside the house, Steve's head popped round the kitchen door with an idiot smile on his face.

'Caught any fish?' snapped Brett. Steve was enough to get on anyone's pip.

'Yeah,' drawled Steve with a broad grin.

'How many?'

'Two,' said Steve. 'Big 'uns.'

'That big?' scoffed Brett holding his thumb and forefinger three centimetres apart.

'Ha ha!' Steve rubbed his cheek against the kitchen doorpost. He had a gleam in his eye that Brett didn't like. Brett stalked past him upstairs.

It was okay! His card was still there in a fold of the duvet where he'd left it when Mark called. Brett snatched it up, but before he could hide it the landing board creaked and there was Steve, pink in the face, peeping round the door.

'Apply Brett Jones!' he spluttered.

'Mind your own business!' Brett yelled furiously. Steve had parked himself on his side of the room. Brett rushed at him like a mad bull, but Steve held him at arm's length and danced as Brett aimed kicks at his legs.

'Apply Brett Jones!' he shrieked.

'What's so funny?' spat Brett.

'Who the hell's going to give you a job?' said Steve, sobering for a moment.

'Why?' demanded Brett.

'Why?' Steve's eyes opened wide. 'Well, how d'you expect anyone to give you a job after all the stupid things you and Mark have done like setting fire to the bracken, Condor's field and...?'

'Shut up!' said Brett, but the anger had gone and he was left feeling weepy and sulky again. 'Darren said,' he whined. 'Darren said I could do it.'

'Yeah, well just don't put your name down,' said Steve. 'Just put your phone number. That way no one will know who you are until it's too late.' He fell back on his bed with his filthy feet on the duvet. He even had fish scales on his T-shirt. 'Just put your phone number,' he giggled. 'And then go along with a Government Health Warning tied to you: THIS BOY COULD SERIOUSLY DAMAGE YOUR HOUSE!'

Brett snorted. Why did he have to be surrounded by thick people who didn't understand? Steve was obsessed with fishing, so why couldn't he paint? He curled up on his bed with his face to the wall. Behind him Steve's bed creaked and a pencil case snapped open.

'Go on,' said Steve's voice. 'Just put your phone number down like this.' He dangled a piece of paper over Brett's ear.

'Huh!' Brett snatched it, crushed it into a ball and threw it over his shoulder. He heard it hit the wall and slide down into the muck at the side of Steve's bed.

'Suit yourself,' Steve said carelessly. The smell of muddy riverbank and fish swept past Brett. Once Steve was safely down in the kitchen, Brett rolled over and lunged across at his brother's bed. He risked slipping his hand into the fluff and filth down the side to get the paper back. He ripped it into tiny pieces, but not before copying it out again slowly and carefully:

PAINTING
Odd jobs evenings and weekends only
£2 an hour
Apply: St.Hermon 316

Chapter 8

The piece of paper sat smoothly inside Brett's back pocket in a folded brown envelope. He couldn't use it without telling Mark – that wouldn't be fair and anyway Mark would go berserk – but beside him Mark was leaning against the school bus window with his eyes half closed. He had dirty tidemarks on his neck. You could always notice them on Mark because his neck was so long and his skin so white.

He knew what he was going to tell Mark. He'd say:

'We've got to get some money for a new tent, Mark.'

They'd lost their other tent in the bracken fire and Mark had already started grumbling that the summer holidays were coming up and they wouldn't be able to go camping. Mark would see the sense in painting, if he knew if was for a tent.

Brett's lips moved, practising.

'What did you say?' demanded Mark, looking down his nose at him.

'Nothing!' Brett flushed.

'You're going bananas,' Mark sniffed. 'That painting yesterday's gone to your brain.' He got up and kicked Brett's leg. It hurt! 'Come on,' he said, 'Let's get out of here.'

Mark elbowed his way out of the bus and stalked off up the road. Brett got out behind Delia Rees. He'd been on the lookout for her anyway.

'Deel!' he said quickly, before the pain in his leg went and he changed his mind.

Delia's thin disgruntled face wrinkled into a smile as soon as she saw it was him. Delia fancied Steve. Brett had told her about his stinking socks and general piggishness, but she still hadn't been put off. Brett pulled the envelope from his pocket and her eyes burnt holes in it. He could see what she was thinking.

'It's a notice,' he said hurriedly.

'Who from?'

'Me.'

'You!' She grabbed hold of it.

'It's just a notice I want you to put up in the village shop,' he hissed in her ear.

She was reading it.

'Who's St. Her...?' She blushed suddenly. 'Who's going to paint?'

'Me.'

'You!'

'Yeah...'

'Why don't you put it up in the shop yourself then?' she asked suspiciously. The sun was shining through her pale frizzy hair and her head looked on fire.

'Because Steve said no one would have me if they knew it was me.'

Her eyes flickered. 'Did Steve ask you to ask me?'

'Yeah,' Brett lied.

Delia responded with an older-sisterly smile. She tapped him on the top of the head with the envelope.

'Okay.'

'Remember!'

''Course I will,' laughed Delia.

Brett went up to school. Mark had disappeared. After the bell went, he found him sitting in class taut as a wire with his head turned to the window. When Mark was in that sort of a state you were scared to touch him in case he crumpled into a heap of dust. Any talk of painting would make him dematerialise completely.

Brett felt a hollow in the pit of his stomach.

'Shall we go down to the river again tonight?' said Brett gruffly. Down at the river they could talk and he could explain.

'Mmm,' said Mark, turning away from the window where the animal shed – Brett's side – stood shiny as a Rolls-Royce showing itself off in the sun.

Mark came for him straight after school before he had finished his tea. Brett stuffed the remains of a sandwich into his mouth and went out to the garage where Mark's front wheel was all but touching the yellow paint tin.

'What's that?' demanded Mark.

'Crap,' mumbled Brett.

'Is your mam painting?'

'It's for the planters,' said Brett swallowing the last of the bread. 'Ainsleigh gave it to her.'

'Ainsleigh!' Mark jeered. 'Ainsleigh!'

'Puky pink and yellow paint.' Brett tried to get Mark to laugh as they pedalled through the village towards the river. If Mark laughed, then he could tell him about the painting. But Mark wasn't listening. He was standing up off his seat with the wind in his hair. He swooped round the corner and vanished down the twisty road.

The riverbank lapped out to meet Brett, mottled brown with pale spikes of green where the new grass was pushing through the burnt ground. All they'd been doing was cooking sausages. The stove had tipped and the flames had wolfed their tent and gone racing across the dry brittle bracken. They were climbing over the hedge into Dan Thomas's field by the time the fire engine had squeezed its way down the lane.

Mark's bike lay in the hedge and Mark himself was picking his way through the burnt grass. Brett jumped over the fence and got his trainers covered in black stuff.

'Shove off!' yelled a voice. It was Steve, who was fishing in the deep pool at the bend. 'Don't come over here.'

'Shove off yourself!' Brett yelled back.

Mark had walked straight into the water in his trainers. He lifted up one foot and let the drips fall down the back of his leg.

'WOO-OW!' He let rip with a yell just to annoy Steve. His arms whirled round in their sockets as he performed a mad dance in the river. Jets of water sprayed his red face and his stary eyes. Centimetre by centimetre his feet edged apart till he sat with a crash in the water.

Brett laughed. He had an acorn-shaped stone in his hand with a thin vein of quartz marking out the cap. He slipped it in his pocket and tossed a pebble up-river. They were a gang again, he and Mark against Steve. It was just a matter of time before they could talk. Mark was sitting in the river pretending to be a fish, his mouth opening and closing.

'Twit!' laughed Brett.

Mark fell forward on all fours and lumbered towards the bank, his stary eyes fixed on Brett.

'Stop it!' giggled Brett. He jumped up and shot back from the gravel into the black stuff that puffed round his ankles.

'Grrr!' Mark was on his feet. Brett turned and ran. Faster still came Mark's legs. He'd got Brett before he reached the green grass at the hedge. 'Arrrrrgh!'

Brett fell flat on his back and got the taste of the black stuff in his mouth.

'Arrgh!' growled Mark grabbing him by the arms.

Brett was dragged giggling and stumbling to the river. Mark's T-shirt had fingerprints all over it. The boys fell into the bubbling current in midstream.

'Arrrgh!' said Mark, shaking himself like a dog.

He crawled through the water on all fours till he got to the bridge where he pulled himself up onto the road. Brett, who couldn't reach, climbed up the bank and through the railings.

'Arrgh!' said Mark, watching.

As Brett dripped towards him, Mark suddenly leapt onto his bike and sped off. By the time Brett reached Greenhill, the only sign of Mark was a trail of wet footprints leading to his front door, followed by a skid mark as if he'd been pulled over the threshold. From inside came the sound of Len Bates shouting and something heavy falling.

Brett scuttled home quickly. Mam was in the kitchen trying to tame some hissing chops. Brett sneaked upstairs in his wet clothes. He'd just had time to dive into the bathroom when the phone rang.

'Brett!' Mam's voice was sharp enough to draw blood.

'Yeah?' Brett whipped off his T-shirt and jeans.

'Brett!'

'What?'

Brett opened the door with a towel round his middle. Mam was almost at the top of the stairs. She ran up to the landing and grabbed him by the shoulder.

'Come on!' she hissed. 'Someone's asking for

a painter.'

Brett lost his towel halfway down the stairs. He tugged it through the banisters. The phone lay on its back on the hall table. He could hear someone breathing at the other end. He snatched it up and left fingerprints all over it.

'Hello.'

The breathing grew louder. 'Is....Is that the painter?' rasped out a voice.

A rush of sweat bubbled out through Brett's bare skin.

'Hello?'

'Hello,' he stammered.

'Is that the painter?'

'Yes.'

The voice wheezed on. Brett's stomach filled with air. Every now and then his voice erupted in a hiccup. When he put down the phone, Mam swam into view like a cardboard cut-out. Her eyebrows rose.

'Who was that?'

'Nelly the elephant,' croaked Brett.

'Oh my God!' gasped Mam. 'You've done it now!'

Chapter 9

Later Mam couldn't stop giggling.

'That'll serve you right for putting notices in shops,' she said, rumpling his still-wet hair.

Steve and Darren were grinning like two apes.

'Nelly the elephant!' hooted Steve.

'Sh!' said Mam. 'Her name's Miss Morris.'

'Did you explain who you were?' asked Darren.

'Yes,' mumbled Brett. That's what made it so creepy, that it had to be Nelly the elephant of all people. And so soon! The others didn't know about Nelly reporting him and Mark. They didn't know about the jumping broad beans.

'And she still wanted you?' said Darren. 'Are you sure she understood who you were?'

'Perhaps she didn't.' Brett turned to Mam. He

wanted Mam to say he couldn't go, but Mam just said:

'Well, you'll see when you go over there, won't you? What time did she say?'

'Seven.' The chop on Brett's plate was making his stomach churn.

'Well, look happy about it,' said Steve.

'He's like his dad,' said Mam with a sarcastic glint in her eye. 'Full of big ideas and then chickening out.'

Brett clenched his teeth and swallowed a piece of meat whole. He wasn't like his dad! His dad was drippy-looking and went round town holding hands with an even bigger drip called Louise. Anyway Dad had left home ten years ago, so he couldn't possibly be like him.

Mam was still watching.

Brett said, 'I don't care.'

'That's okay, baby,' said Mam, 'because you're going anyway. You've promised.' After another mouthful of potato, she asked, 'Mark isn't going, is he?'

'No.' Brett dropped his knife and fork. He couldn't eat any more. He'd have to get over to Nelly's without Mark seeing him.

'There's hopes then,' Mam said.

Mam, Darren and Steve kept on hanging around him. They were getting on his nerves. His heart was thumping worse than if he were going to jump into a crocodile pit. Darren even thought he was wearing his school trousers to create a good impression.

'Good man,' he said. 'You've got to look smart.'

'My jeans are wet, stupid!' he said through his teeth.

'Oh!' Darren looked surprised. He never put a foot wrong now he had a girlfriend and a job. He was really sick.

'Don't tell Mark I've gone to Nelly's. Not yet, okay?' Brett said hurriedly.

'Right.'

'Tell Mam and Steve not to.'

'Okay.'

Brett gave them the slip. When they were all in the front room, he went out through the back, round the garage, over the hedge and into the lane beyond. They'd just have to go on waiting. He'd be back in two ticks anyway. He wasn't going to stay long enough to be trampled by Nelly the elephant once she recognised him.

He sucked in his breath in tiny mouthfuls which kept getting stuck in his throat. His chest was bursting by the time he got to Nelly's. He'd only just touched her gate, when the front door opened and there she was like a giant black hole sucking him in.

Brett had never stopped and looked at her properly before and he didn't look now. He stared at a spot to the right of the door whilst she spoke in an odd voice that sounded as if a gallon of oil had been poured on her usual bark.

'The painter, is it?' she called. She hadn't opened her mouth far enough and the words were skidding over her teeth.

'Yes,' grunted Brett.

'Come on in.'

Brett could have sworn the pathway moved under his feet. Her huge shadow just kept getting closer and closer. He saw her hand let go of the door and grope like a crab for something on a tall spindly cupboard just behind her.

'I saw your notice in the shop,' said Nelly the elephant. Now her voice was floating in the top of her throat. 'Two pounds an hour, isn't it?'

'Yes,' said Brett.

He'd reached her doorstep. Her finger was beckoning him in. He was breathing in the musty air of the house. She must be able to recognise him now. Even the broad bean plants could see him. There they were jigging about beyond the kitchen window at the end of the passageway, their smudgy dark eyes all agog. They wanted to see him cop it in the neck for making three of their mates jump out of the soil.

Brett glanced at the elephant at last.

'I'm Brett Jones,' he said stonily. 'From the estate.'

Nelly the elephant nodded. There was a funny sort of shine in her eyes that should have warned him.

'The egg man,' she said.

'Pardon?'

'The egg man.'

Abruptly her fingers opened to show the egg-shaped stone. The chick was still there amid the triangular cracks.

'Did you throw this into my garden?' asked Nelly

the elephant.

Brett stepped back. In a matter of seconds all sorts of excuses whirled around his head and burned out. He nodded dumbly.

'Good good good good,' said Nelly the elephant.

Brett's neck jerked. Nelly's grey face came right up to him. It was shinier than the rest of her. Her hair clung like steel wire to her head and formed a knot at the back too small for a bun. A funny rusty chuckle bubbled up from inside her.

'I want you to change my front room into an egg,' said Nelly the elephant.

The world stood still. Then something clicked in Brett's brain. She was mad! Mad! Suddenly he wanted to giggle too.

'A Fabergé egg,' said Nelly the elephant.

A fabber jay egg!

Mark would never believe this! He'd bust himself laughing.

Nelly the elephant shuffled round and the bulk of her body forced him to retreat into the front room behind the window with the twitchy curtains. He caught sight of himself – small, red-faced, spiky blond-haired and about to explode – in the mirror that hung at an angle over the castiron fireplace. He saw the mouldy wallpaper too, all brown and spotty and egg-like. At the top of the mirror were Nelly the elephant's eyes watching him.

'How can you change a room into an egg?' he burst out.

'I'll bring some pictures to show you,' said Nelly the elephant.

Her fingers opened and closed round the stone. Brett held out his hand to stop her blurring the lines, but she slipped the stone into the safety of her pocket. Nelly's Exhibit A: stone thrown by Brett Jones.

'Of course,' she went on, 'Ted Morgan has offered to do it many times – he helps me with the garden already – but I wanted someone with more...'

Brett caught his breath. She let the word float towards him, teasing. More...

'I wanted someone with more imagination who could take this room and make it look bright and different,' said Nelly the elephant calmly, 'so anyone passing by will turn towards the window and have a surprise.'

She couldn't mean him!

'You can do it, can't you?' she said.

'You want me to paint?' his voice burst out.

'Yes.'

Brett fixed his eyes on her face. Couldn't she see who she was talking to – Brett Jones, aged twelve, the guy who'd got her broad beans? And all this talk about eggs...

'You want me to paint this room?' he asked breathlessly.

'Yes.'

His neck cricked as he tried to make himself look around him.

'I want you to paint this room so it looks good from

outside,' said Nelly the elephant. Before the words could sink in, a car stopped outside and she began to move in between the plasticky chairs and the tinkling china cupboard with its thin damp plates. She reached the window and lifted the net curtain just as Ray Condor jumped out of his land-rover. A shiver of sunlight flashed into the room, nailed Brett to the wall and blinded him. When he opened his eyes, Ray Condor was coming towards the window with a sack on his back.

Nelly the elephant let go of the curtain and rumbled out of the room. Ray Condor beat her to the front door. There came the thump of the falling sack, followed by hammering. As soon as the door opened, the stink of cow dung flowed right into the house.

'Miss Morris?' Ray Condor gasped. 'Miss Morris, are you all right?'

Brett felt Ray Condor's eyes trying to deflect into the front room. He'd been trapped! It was all a trick. He was going to cop it all on his own without Mark.

'I've had some boys in my cornfield and I thought...'

'It's all right. My painter's here,' the elephant said in her oily voice.

'Who?' gasped Ray Condor.

Brett couldn't believe his ears either.

'Just my painter,' the elephant said.

Chapter 10

Her painter!

It sounded brill, even if 'her' was Nelly the elephant.

All next morning Brett kept on turning over in his mind the arrangements Nelly'd made with him once she'd seen Condor off. She'd talked to him about undercoat and gloss as if he were a real painter like Ainsleigh. At the thought of it Brett felt sweaty and kept on wanting to giggle. That's why he didn't trust himself to speak first. He wanted Mark to ask him instead, 'Where were you last night then?' Then he'd explain how Nelly the stupid old elephant had actually saved him from Ray Condor and now he was going to paint for her for two pounds an hour. He didn't mention the egg, though, because he didn't understand what the egg was all about, except that it made him feel as though he were standing on tiptoe like a UFO ready for take-off.

But Mark didn't ask a thing. It was Cannon who asked when 7B were filing out after registration.

'Brett,' he said. 'Do you do any painting at home?'

'No,' said Brett.

'I thought perhaps you helped your mam.'

'Mam won't let me,' said Brett.

'Oh!' Cannon laughed. 'You did a good job on that shed, Brett,' he said reaching for his briefcase and pushing his chair back. 'Keep it up. Good lad. That's what I like to see.'

Mark was waiting at the foot of the stairs.

'What did he want?'

'Wanted to know if I did any painting at home.' Brett shrugged.

'You!'

'Well, I could.'

'Creep! Tell him to mind his stupid business,' Mark said angrily.

'Well, I could if I wanted to get money for a tent,' Brett said, but Mark had gone.

After tea Mark went up to town with his mother without saying a word. Brett heard the car and watched it go from behind the curtains of his bedroom window. Mark still hadn't come back when Mam fished out a too-small pair of jeans from the back of the airing cupboard.

'You can always put in a pin to hold them,' she said

to Brett. 'And pull your T-shirt down over it. No use ruining a good pair of jeans, which you would, knowing you.'

She wouldn't let go of the jeans for a minute.

'Are you sure Miss Morris wants you?' she asked.

'Yeah,' said Brett spikily.

'And you're going to paint her front room?'

'She must be mad!' said Steve. He and Darren were standing around gawping.

'No, she's not,' said Brett. He wasn't going to let Steve think she was mad, even if he had doubts himself.

'Bet you won't last two days,' said Steve.

'Now Brett, if the work's too difficult for you, you tell her,' Mam said anxiously. 'Don't you go being silly and letting her down. If you do, I'll . . .'

Brett escaped from his mam's gritting teeth. He slipped over the hedge again and raced along the main road, so Mark wouldn't come back from town and catch him. He wanted to see Nelly too to check he hadn't been dreaming.

If he had, why was she standing on the doorstep waiting? First thing he saw as he dived past her into the passageway was the egg-shaped stone sitting in style on the spindly cupboard. Then he spotted the tin of paint on the floor of the front room.

'Ted Morgan took me up to town this morning and I got the paint,' she said. 'White undercoat just as you told me.'

Brett looked at her quickly. Yes, she was serious. On

the lev. It was mad. He couldn't get his breath for a moment. There was her and Cannon treating him as if he were six feet tall and shaving. Perhaps it was the green paint that had done it. Perhaps he hadn't just painted the animal shed, he'd painted himself as well and they couldn't recognise him. Perhaps he was a green giant and wouldn't recognise himself! Before he could check in the front room mirror, Nelly said, 'And I got this,' and edged him towards the kitchen.

Brett trod warily down the passageway, in case there was a man-eating lion – or worse still, Ray Condor – waiting for him at the far end. But when he got there, the kitchen was okay. Yeah! He drew in a deep breath and let it out slowly. It was quite cosy, a bit like his gran's kitchen, full of painted cupboards with lumpy-patterned glass doors except that Nelly's cupboards were green and she had two easy chairs by the table piled high with cushions. Instead of a man-eating lion a stout bear in red wellies and flat cap sat on one of the chairs.

'That's Grumpus,' said Nelly.

The bear looked like a shrunken farmer. Brett giggled so suddenly that the pin that was holding his jeans pinged. He was trying to close it one-handed when Nelly took out a book from the drawer of the kitchen table. He watched warily as she slid it towards him.

'Wow!' Brett let go of the pin when he saw the picture on the front.

'Fabergé eggs,' Nelly said.

Brett stared. A dribble of spit trickled over his lower lip and hung there. He caught it just before it plopped onto an egg. It wasn't a bird's egg at all, but an egg made of pure gold, a shining egg with a door in its side that opened into a tiny sparkling cave.

'Fabergé used to make them for the Russian kings – the tsars,' Nelly said gruffly. 'They used to give them to the family as Easter gifts.'

Fabergé was a man! Brett took the pages in his hand. Then with a glance to make sure that Nelly approved and holding his breath so as not to disturb them, he let the golden eggs spring out carefully one by one. They were more brilliant than anything he'd ever seen. He caught the very last and ran his fingers over the fragile bird that flew inside.

'Do you understand what I want you to do?' Nelly asked.

'Mm?' Another dribble escaped. It fell in a foamy pool on the back of his hand and he wiped it against his jeans.

'Ted Morgan says my house looks so grey and run down from the outside, that's why the village children throw stones at it,' Nelly said matter-of-factly. 'He says if the house was painted, people wouldn't take advantage. Well, I can't afford to have the whole house painted, that's why I thought of the Fabergé egg.'

Brett raised his eyes and blinked at her. Nelly was eyeing him. Two bright pink spots glowed on her cheeks. Now that she was close, her face didn't seem so very big at all. It was the rest of her body that was huge and even that was stooping towards him. Her shoulder was barely above the height of his own. He felt quite safe even though she was talking about the village kids.

'I thought,' said Nelly the elephant in a gruff voice, 'I thought if I had this one room shining out like the inside of an egg, it would do just as well. People will see it and then they won't notice the grey walls around it. Do you understand?'

Brett gazed down at the jewelled egg beneath his hand and made it change into Nelly's grey house with a golden window.

'Yes,' he said.

He did too, but some seconds went by before he realised she was waiting. He looked up with a jerk.

'I don't know if I can do it,' he gasped, panic-struck. 'I've only ever painted . . . '

'Yes?'

'An animal shed.' He flushed to the roots of his hair. 'I've only painted an animal shed. Mam won't let me paint.'

'But you want to,' said Nelly the elephant.

'Yes!' The word burst out in a bubble that floated away, shone like a rainbow.

'I thought as much,' smiled Nelly the elephant, straightening till her shoes creaked. 'When I saw two pounds an hour, I knew it was someone who really wanted to paint. You can't get anyone to work for that sort of money now. I pay Ted three pounds an hour to do my garden, although he doesn't want anything. But I don't think Ted would like the idea of a Fabergé egg.'

The skin of her hands looked as if it had worn thin. Brett's eyes travelled up to her face. This old woman was going to give him a room, a whole room, when Ainsleigh'd only given him a piddling aeroplane and Mam a pair of planters. She was giving him a whole room, if he wanted to take it.

'Well,' she said, before he could chicken out. 'It's seven twenty-three. We'd better start with the ceiling.'

Everything was ready for him, the paint, the stepladder, the plasticky chairs and table pushed back. The room ponged of dirty water where Nelly'd wiped the paintwork with a mop.

Nelly picked up the tin of paint and stood waiting at the foot of the ladder, while he climbed up. He was just reaching down for the paint when he felt a stab of pain in his belly.

'Pin!' he yelped.

A startled Nelly laughed and watched him snap it shut and bunch his T-shirt into the top of his jeans behind it. She slid the tin onto the ladder with lizardy fingers. A brush lay across it. It was Brett's third brand new brush in three days.

As soon as he gripped the brush, Brett's shoulder tensed. Nelly was watching him hungrily with her fingers still clutching the stepladder. He wanted to tell her that you shouldn't expect too much of undercoat, but instead a funny nervous giggle ran through him like an electric current and he had to grit his teeth to stop it jumping out.

He dipped his brush in the paint, but his shoulder was so stiff he couldn't get it out again. Perhaps all that painting on the shed had done his arm in. He was just beginning to panic, when his elbow cricked. His arm rose as though on a spring and left the first dab of paint, brilliant white on the ceiling.

Brett clutched his sore muscles.

'All right?' asked Nelly in her normal voice that was deeper than his dad's.

'Yes,' he gasped, though he wasn't sure.

Nelly drew back. The house itself grew still and outside seemed a million miles away. The sun was sliding down behind the rooftops opposite. As Brett nerved himself for another stab at the paint, a ray reached out from between the chimney pots and darted across the ceiling to help him. When the ray touched the white dab, it burned up like a star. Brett dipped his brush quickly into the paint and, following the line of the sun, made the white star grow and grow.

He didn't dare stop. He went on spreading the rays of the star across the ceiling as fast as his arms could go. When he had to move the stepladder, he jumped down, tugged it across and scrambled back up again all in one breath. He painted steadily in between the rays, moving a sea of white across the room. A mist of paint drifted onto his head. The brush had stuck to the sore bit on his finger. It was like an extra hand reaching into the farthest corners.

'Steady!' Nelly's voice murmured close by him.

Brett felt the stepladder rock and didn't care. It was almost done. He'd reached the window and his brush was delving into the dark spaces above the pelmet.

'Steady!'

Nelly was holding the stepladder. It rocked back into place.

'Finished!'

Brett stopped at last, breathed out and opened his arms. Behind him stretched a vast expanse of startling white. It was like a miracle. He'd done it! On his own he'd done it! He stood up tall with the ceiling on his shoulders, whilst Nelly trundled out of the room and out of the front door.

He knew he'd done okay, but he knew it even more when he saw her face. She'd gone to stand in the middle of the lawn and she was grinning at him so daftly that he couldn't help but giggle.

Then he saw Mark behind her cycling along the road from the direction of Greenhill.

Chapter 11

'I got myself a job,' Brett said straight out. He felt tall enough to confront Mark – after all he'd painted a ceiling. They were at the bus-stop. Mark was staring into space. 'I just want some money to get us a tent.'

'I though you *just* wanted to paint your hair,' Mark cut in with a grin that made the vein on his temple stand out. He flicked Brett's hair as he stepped past him to get to the bus. 'Twit!' he said over his shoulder.

Mark went to sit with Winffie and Tim in the back leaving Brett to take the last empty seat next to Jenny Williams who kept staring.

'You've got paint in your hair,' she said as soon as the bus stopped at the school gate.

Brett ignored her. He left the bus with the first wave

of bodies so it wouldn't look as if he were walking up to school on his own.

Cannon spotted his hair too. It was as if Nelly'd marked him with the letters NE, property of Nelly the Elephant. He scratched at his hair like mad till Davina turned round.

'Have you got nits, Brett Jones?' she asked bossily.

Mark laughed. Brett kicked her chair then hid behind her as Cannon reappeared for an English lesson. Normally Cannon never noticed him unless he made a noise, but the trouble with being tall was that Cannon could spot him without any trouble at all. And Cannon kept on smiling at Brett as though he had golden eggs sprouting out of his head.

At the end of the lesson Cannon said: 'Right! I want you all to write a poem, an essay, a story or whatever you like by next Monday – on painting.'

Brett sank lower. Why did Cannon have to? And why was it that only people like Cannon and Nelly understood about his painting? Beside him Mark's taut knuckles gripped the edge of the desk.

'Painting!' squealed Nia.

'What sort of painting?' grumbled Claire.

'Just painting,' said Cannon amiably. 'Any sort of painting at all.' He ignored Nia's groan. 'We've got two painters in the class after all.'

'Huh!' the girls erupted.

'Only one, sir,' called out Mark. 'I'm not one.' His voice could have cut through stone.

Mark stayed in a glittery-sharp mood. Being near him was like rubbing up against sandpaper. Brett knew that without saying a word Mark was trying to psyche him out of painting for Nelly. He'd never felt Mark psyche him before however much Mam tried to claim that Mark made him do things he didn't want to do. He watched Mark from the corner of his eye. He wasn't going to give up on his egg. Mark couldn't do anything to him. Anyway Nelly's painting was only going to last a few more days.

After school Mark called round on his board. He skated off to the playground and, when Brett caught up, he was standing his skateboard on the middle of the seesaw. Barry Ellis, Steve's friend, had gone smashing to the ground and broken his elbow doing that last year.

Mark though climbed up and stood tall, taller than the swings and the climbing frame, and dead still. Just when the stillness was getting too much, Mark let out a blood-curdling yell. The seesaw tipped and sent the skateboard crashing against the iron hand-hold. Mark had already leapt off. He gathered up the somersaulting skateboard and skated across the tarmac. Brett, with his pulse racing, skated after him out onto the pavement where they raced Mam's Metro home.

'Idiot!' Mam gasped pink-faced to Brett when the car stopped. 'You were making me nervous. I thought I was going to crash into you.'

Mark grinned and bunny-hopped onto the lawn.

Mam set her lips in a thin line.

'Supper at six-fifteen prompt,' she said. 'Don't be late.'

Her voice sliced the evening in two. Mark spun round on his board and caught the tail end of the meaningful glance she directed at Brett. Brett retreated into the garage where he rumbled slowly in a square. Mark rumbled in after him. They made a noise like empty wagons in a station till Mark jumped off and sat astride his board. He had a fizzy electric air about him that was trying to frazzle Brett up. Brett wasn't having that either. He watched Mark roll his board over to Ainsleigh's tins of paint.

'Let's have a butcher's,' said Mark.

'It's just paint,' said Brett.

'It's just paint,' mimicked Mark.

Brett got the chisel out of the old food cupboard and prised open the yellow tin.

'Ugh!' said Mark. 'Guess what that reminds me of.'

'I know,' said Brett. He opened the pink tin.

'Reminds me of Ainsleigh,' said Mark. 'Vomit.'

He picked up the paintbrush that Brett had left balanced on the tins and dabbed Brett's hair with it.

'Don't!'

'Don't you want me to paint?'

'You don't want to paint,' said Brett.

'Right on,' said Mark twirling his board and skating off up the road.

The skateboard lay across the pavement to trip him

up. It was Mark's idea of a joke. Brett stepped over it, but he got an itchy feeling in his back all the way to Nelly's as if someone were watching him.

The itchiness went as soon as he got to Nelly's gate and saw the front room ceiling soar up and up into infinite space. He wanted to lie down on the lawn – just as Ainsleigh had done when he was painting his pond fence – and stare at it. He would have too, if Nelly hadn't come to the window and blotted it out. Brett waved at her and grinned stupidly.

Nelly the elephant bustled to the front door.

'Isn't it good?' she called.

'It's eggstraordinary,' grinned Brett.

It took a while for her brain to creak into action. When she understood, she laughed and at once Brett felt a ray of white light reach out of the front room and touch him on the shoulder. Arise, Sir Brett Jones! You made her laugh. It was amazing what unknown things he could do.

He could even fool a bear! He swaggered down the passageway to the kitchen and winked at Grumpus who peeped at him slyly from beneath his cap. Grumpus probably thought that he, Brett, was someone really important, someone with a van like Ainsleigh's who'd painted loads and loads of houses. Nelly bent Grumpus forward in a sort of bow and plucked out a bag from behind his back.

'Hand over, Grumpus lad,' she said.

Her fingers were stiff and wouldn't do what she wanted. Brett waited patiently, feeling Christmassy again. He felt more Christmassy still when Nelly tipped up the bag and out fell half a dozen cards with little rectangles of different coloured paints.

'What do you think, Mr Painter?' smiled Nelly the elephant.

'What?' said Brett. He was running his itchy fingers over the little squares of paint.

'I want you to choose the colours for the front room. If you finish with the undercoat tonight, we'll need the proper shades tomorrow.' Her face shone like oiled paper as she waited for his reply.

'I'll finish,' Brett said confidently.

'Which ones then?' asked Nelly, shuffling round in front of the table.

'I wouldn't mind all of them,' sighed Brett. 'Except . . . ' He stabbed his finger on an Ainsleigh pink and an Ainsleigh yellow. 'Except these.'

The elephant chuckled. It came from deep inside her rusty brown dress that tied at the back and was decorated with white flowers hardly bigger than dots. Brett looked up. He never thought she could have giggled like that. And she'd believed him too!

'They sell lots of tiny tins of paint,' she said eagerly. 'We could get lots . . . '

'No.' It was Brett's turn to laugh. 'I didn't mean it. If we got lots of colours, it would look spotty and horrible.' He told her about Steve's half of bedroom with the blobs of Blu-tack. 'We've got to choose just one colour,' he explained. 'Or maybe two.'

His fingers lingered over a pale green that would

have looked just right for his own room whilst behind Nelly's back something pinged against the woodshed roof, trickled gently along the furrows of the zinc, paused and dropped. From the ground came a softer echoing ping that trickled like a kindly thought through Brett's brain. He turned the paint card round and slid it over to Nelly.

'It's your room,' he said generously. 'You choose.'

'No, you're the one who's going to see it from outside,' countered Nelly, pulling her hand away.

'But it's still your room and you thought about the egg and everything,' Brett said.

A faint smile came to Nelly's face and tugged at the wrinkles round the corners of her mouth. She couldn't believe she'd thought of the golden egg. It was pretty unbelievable.

'You did!' said Brett, more to remind himself than her.

Nelly replied with a half-burp, half-chuckle.

'Come on,' coaxed Brett. 'Choose a colour.' He settled himself comfortably beside her, half-lying on the table with his nose almost touching the paint card. It was brill. Fancy someone asking for his advice. Mam, Steve, Darren and Mark always knew everything.

He watched Nelly's fingers slide over the coloured squares and stop at the very green he'd chosen for himself. She was copying him. He looked up at her and shook his head.

'It doesn't look eggy,' he said.

Nelly pursed her lips.

'It doesn't,' said Brett. 'It's nice, though. That's the colour I'm going to have in my room when Darren moves out.'

'Wasn't it Steve?' countered Nelly.

'No. Well, Darren first.' Brett laughed. She must be really listening to him and taking in every word he said. He took time to explain to her that Darren had to get a flat in town before Steve could move out of the room they shared.

'Darren?' said Nelly. 'Isn't he the one who waits for the bus on Saturday mornings? Smart boy.'

'Yuck!' cried Brett. Then, 'He's okay,' he conceded. 'Most of the time. It's when he's fussy and bigheaded he gets on my nerves. He works in the supermarket in Laurel Street.'

Nelly knew that too. Brett rubbed his stomach against the edge of the table and eyed her. It was funny how much she knew – and he didn't know her at all. Even when he was nobbling her broad beans she must have known about him. He glanced at the window and saw the privet in the side hedge shake.

Almost at once another something pinged against the woodshed roof. This time he felt it force its way down inside him like a too-big sweet. Mark wasn't going to let him paint for Nelly without a fight. He was outside in the hedge.

Above him Nelly's voice said: 'Cream pearl?'

Her fingers had come to a halt on a square of rich cream shot through with pearly lights. She was asking his opinion, but Brett couldn't speak. All his senses were fixed on the hail of pebbles that came flying over the hedge and spat across the back yard behind the kitchen door.

'Cream pearl?' repeated Nelly in her skiddy voice. 'Cream pearl for the skirting, door and window-sills?'

She touched his stiff shoulder. Brett shot back onto the floor.

'Yes,' he said breathlessly. ''Snice.'

Quivers were running up and down his back as if each and every pebble had struck a nerve.

'What about the ceiling?' Nelly asked.

A larger stone drowned her voice. It ran along the woodshed roof. A second's silence, an intake of breath, followed by an echoing thud on the cement below.

'White?' She was talking to herself.

'With a touch of lemon,' gasped Brett, turning his scared face towards her.

Nelly looked for the paint.

'White with a hint of lemon,' she read out. 'I'll write it down.'

At last Nelly let go of the table. She put her hand on Grumpus's head and eased her way in between the chairs to the kitchen cupboard. She was trying to slide her fingers round the cupboard door, when a handful of earth rattled against the kitchen window. Brett spun round and through the trickling dirt saw Mark at the side hedge with his arm in the air.

'Get lost!' he mouthed savagely. 'GET LOST!'

His only answer was a fusillade of pebbles that

seemed to come flying straight for him. He swung away and pressed his back hard against the sink to shield Nelly who was coming towards him with a notebook in her hand. Nelly stopped.

'Hang on a minute!' Brett dashed past her to the kitchen door. It had hardly opened when he heard Mark's footsteps run for the road. He drew his sleeve over his mouth and closed the door again quickly. For a moment he stood with his hand on the latch, too ashamed to turn round.

But behind him Nelly's voice spelled out as if nothing had happened, 'Cream . . . pearl . . . for the woodwork . . . and for the ceiling white . . . with a hint of lemon.'

Chapter 12

That was what he liked about painting. You could cover mucky old wood and anything that annoyed you. You could even cover over Mark. By the time Brett had got round the skirting as far as the door the shaky feeling in his arms had gone. Mark was just a stupid idiot. It was as if he were looking down from the top of a stepladder and seeing Mark as he'd never seen him before. When that happened he slowed down so as to enjoy the sweep of the bristles over the old chipped wood. Nelly was humming out in the kitchen and no more stones landed on the roof.

Da da da dum dum. Brett had picked up the tune and was humming his way home, when the front wheel of Mark's bike slid though the playground hedge and Mark's face leered at him through the thin branches.

'Leave her alone,' said Brett in the long-suffering voice his mam sometimes used with him.

'Leave her alone,' mimicked Mark.

'I don't think she told Condor about us, you know.'

'I don't think she told Condor about us, you know.'

'She knew you were there anyway,' Brett said. 'She just wasn't bothered, that's all.'

That bit of information made Mark cycle off across the playground. Da da da dum dum. Brett thought he was going home, but Mark swung round, waited, then kept pace with him.

'My dad says Nelly the elephant's a mean old cow,' said Mark after a while. 'When he was working for her, she didn't even offer him a cup of tea.'

'She gave me a fiver.' Brett produced it from his pocket and brandished it in front of Mark's nose. Nelly'd gone upstairs to get it while he was painting the top part of the door. He'd heard the squeak of a drawer and the rattle of coins directly above him as though someone were pouring money on his head.

'Big deal,' said Mark. 'A lousy fiver. Where'd she keep it? In a potty under her bed?'

Brett looked round sharply. Mark laughed.

'Bet it's wet and smelly,' he said. 'Bet it's been pissed on.'

'I'm going to get us a tent,' snapped Brett.

'For you and Nelly? Wow!'

'We've got to get one before the summer holidays,' Brett said through his teeth. 'You and me.'

'I can get one without having to do some stupid

painting,' scoffed Mark.

'How?' demanded Brett.

Mark cycled round him, grinning and tapping his nose, then sent his bike skidding towards his own garage door.

'You can't!' Brett yelled after him.

Mam was out brushing the floor of the car. She took one glance at Brett's red face.

'Mark wasn't bothering you, was he?' she asked.

'No.'

'Remember you're a workman now. You've got responsibilities.'

'Mam!' Brett snorted. He went into the house and slammed the door. Why couldn't Mam and Mark just let him get on with things without any fuss? Why couldn't they?

The questions in his head made him toss and turn all night. The very next morning he went down to the shop before the bus came and took his card out of the window.

Brett ripped up the card and stuffed the bits in the hedge. It wasn't fair. Painting or no painting, Mark always got his own way in the end.

It wasn't fair. He felt soft as a snail without its shell when he went round to Nelly's in the evening and watched her lever the lid off a brand new paint tin and hold up a lemon moon. He'd been staring at the moon so long without so much as a smile that it slipped from Nelly's hand and made him jump. Nelly snatched it up and wiped the paint off the sink with a J-cloth.

'Anything wrong?' she asked gruffly over her shoulder.

'No,' said Brett. He hadn't meant to show her he was in a mood. It wasn't her fault. And he was still going to finish his contract with her, even if he had taken his card from the window.

'Are you sure you want to paint tonight?' she asked in a thick voice.

'Yes,' said Brett. 'Yes, I do,' he insisted when he saw the flicker of disappointment on her face. 'I want to do it.'

He moved across from the table which was making a dent in his backside and tried to pick up the tin, but her fingers closed round the handle and she wouldn't let go.

'It's okay,' he said. 'I'm not fed up. Mam says I start things and then chicken out, but I don't. It's just other people bugging me.'

'Who?' said Nelly.

'People who don't think I can do things on my own,' grumbled Brett, slumping against the sink.

'Well, do you think you can?' Nelly asked.

Brett sniffed. 'Do you?' he muttered.

'Yes.'

Her voice sounded wrong. Brett allowed himself to look at her carefully from under his lashes. She was grinning all over her face.

'How do you know?' he demanded angrily. She didn't know anything about him.

Nelly pointed mischievously at a photograph of three faces on the wall beside the kitchen cupboard. It was a cracked old photograph that looked as if it had been made out of a jigsaw.

'Yes,' she repeated. 'In fact I know if there's any one person who can do it, it's you.'

Brett frowned. If she was taking the mick . . . He curled his fingers round the edge of the draining board. In the shiny surface he watched his face getting redder. What was she on about? He glanced quickly over his shoulder and saw that the photograph had an oval frame. It must be eggs again. The eggs had gone to her brain. Out in the passageway she'd even put the egg-stone to stand on a round lacy mat. She must think it was a mysterious message from outer space and not just a stone he'd scribbled on while waiting for Mark to nobble her beans.

'Have you been talking to my mam?' he asked suddenly.

'Your mam? No.' Behind him Nelly shook her head. 'Well at least, not recently. We do exchange a few words sometimes when we meet in the shop.'

That wasn't what he meant. Anyway the idea was daft. Mam wouldn't have got Nelly to ask him to paint. She would never have risked it.

He reached awkwardly for the tin and this time Nelly let go of it. He could feel her smiling at the top of his head as he carried it off to the front room. She didn't follow. Egg-stone or whatever, it must mean she trusted him.

Brett sat the tin on the ladder. Once he'd got his breath and cooled down, he climbed up after it and dipped his brush extravagantly in the paint. Then he stretched right out and made the paint follow him across the ceiling smooth as butter. He looked back at it with a contented sniff. No wonder Ainsleigh was always in a good mood. Painting was bound to make you feel ace. After a while his shoulders relaxed and he started to hum. Mark's dad was an electrician and that was different. The sparks had got into his blood and Mark's too.

It was as he was thinking of Mark that he heard a commotion at the gate. His brush went berserk and zigzagged across the ceiling. Brett ducked below the level of the pelmet and saw it was only Ted Morgan getting out of his car with the local paper in his hand. Quickly he painted over the zigzag before Ted came busybodying up the path. He couldn't let Nelly down in front of him.

He carried on painting even when the letterbox clicked and Ted went past the window. He painted steadily to make a good impression. It was just like pulling a silken yellow curtain over yesterday's grey. As soon as Ted's footsteps had died away round the side of the house, he heard Nelly creep up the passage and pick up the paper. She didn't come in.

Brett swung his arms to let the blood flow, then worked his way carefully back and forth across the room to check for pale bits. When he was satisfied that no one else would see any either, he carried the paint tin back to the kitchen and beamed at Nelly who was sitting at the table behind the local paper.

Nelly put the paper down.

'Ted Morgan's outside,' she said in a low voice.

'Yeah,' said Brett calmly.

So what? His ceiling was good enough for anyone – even Ted who was bending behind the broad beans and spreading Ray Condor's sack of dung on a freshly dug patch of garden. The sun polished up his red skin. As soon as he saw Brett at the window, he dropped his fork and began to advance across the grass with his hands hanging like hams at his side.

Nelly gripped the edge of the table and tried to pull herself up in a hurry, but Ted's boots were already crushing the pebbles on the apron of cement round the back door. He opened the door before Nelly could get to it. Brett was in the middle of wiping his fingers with a turps-soaked rag. He finished the job before turning to meet Ted's stare man to man.

''llo,' said Brett.

'Brett's just finished the ceiling,' Nelly said in a toady voice.

Ted grunted. The trouble with Ted was that he had no sense of humour. Brett made a show of dunking the brush in a baked bean tin half full of turps.

'Would you like to see it?' Nelly asked.

The kitchen flags squealed. Ted's boots would have crushed eggshells to dust. They echoed down the passageway till they came to the door of the front room. Silence. Brett waited smugly. His painting had taken Ted's breath away!

'Brett's very good and keen,' began Nelly. 'He . . . '

'He should have stripped the paper first,' said Ted Morgan.

'Pardon?'

'Before painting he should have stripped the paper.'

Brett's face screwed up. The heavy feet came tramping back towards him.

'Should have stripped the paper,' ground the voice.

Big-headed git, said Brett in his mind. Nelly hadn't told him to strip the paper. It wasn't his fault. She'd know that, Nelly would.

'Behaving yourself, are you?' Ted placed himself squarely behind Brett and Brett felt shivers running up and down his neck. Ted was a squat man, not that much taller than himself, but he had this way sometimes of clamping his hand round the backs of boys' necks which he thought was friendly. Ted wasn't being friendly now.

Brett straightened.

'Yes, he's been very good,' said Nelly. 'He . . . '

'I saw you and those other boys hanging around Ray Condor's gate the other day,' grunted Ted, ignoring her and addressing Brett's back. 'When I was going past in the car.'

Brett bared his teeth. Ha, so he was right! Nelly hadn't grassed on them to Condor. It was Ted who'd done it, probably over a sack of dung.

'Hope you drop in a cowpat,' he said under his breath.

'Pardon?' said Ted.

'Nothing,' said Brett politely.

Ted stood his ground. He wasn't finished.

'What are those chippings?' he asked.

'Chippings?' echoed Nelly.

A chipping squealed beneath Ted's feet.

'All over the back yard,' he said.

Nelly followed him out and the door swung to behind them. Brett scratched at a blob of paint on his finger. Ted was jealous. He didn't have any imagination, Nelly'd said so. Nelly didn't care about the chippings, only the painting. Brett wiped his hands and marched noisily down the passage to show he didn't have to listen to the drone of Ted's voice if he didn't want to.

He dropped down on the bottom stair and pressed his face against the banister till he looked like a gargoyle in the front room mirror. The gargoyle poked its tongue out at Ted Morgan. By the time the kitchen door opened and Nelly came bustling in, Brett had two deep dents running down his cheeks.

He got up and hung over the banister, so she could tell him what thicko Ted had said, but she didn't breathe a word. Instead he saw her scared eyes skim like bluebottles up the stairs. Brett jumped back as if they'd stung him.

'What's he been telling you?' he cried. 'I haven't been upstairs!'

'No!' Nelly got a grip on herself. 'No, no,' she said hurriedly. 'No. It wasn't anything like that.'

But she was lying. Brett knew it. Ted Morgan had told her to watch him in case he pinched her money. Brett blundered towards the front door.

'Brett!' cried Nelly.

'I've got to go home,' he said hotly.

'Brett!' she warned.

Brett stopped. Her voice was the voice of the Nelly he knew before he'd started painting. When he turned to face her, he felt himself go back to being small and miserable.

Her voice dropped.

'And what if Ted did say that?' she said breathlessly. 'I don't have to believe it. You mustn't let him put you off.'

'I'm not frightened.' He was whining again, but it wasn't just the money. Nothing was ever as simple as he wanted it to be. He slumped against the wall and watched Nelly shuffle off to the kitchen. She came back and stood at the door of the front room with the egg book in her hand.

'Here. Take it,' she said. 'It's for you I bought it.'

Brett stared from the book to the room behind her. In that moment he saw what Ted had seen – mouldy wallpaper and yucky furniture drowning out his bit of paint. He just hadn't a hope of ever changing that room into a perfect golden egg.

Chapter 13

No one could make a golden egg with just a bit of paint.

Brett brooded on it all next day, while Mark fooled around with Winffie and Tim. Thicko Ted was right. Nelly's room would look crap until it had new carpets and furniture and everything else. Why hadn't she thought of that? She was either daft or she was having him on.

'Brett,' said Mam at the supper table. 'Is anything wrong?'

'No,' said Brett.

'Are you going to Miss Morris's tonight?'

'Yeah.'

He got up from the table before she could ask him any more questions. Anyway first he had to find out what Nelly was playing at.

He went over the hedge as a matter of course, though he knew Mark had gone down to the village to Winffie and Tim. He raced along the road and hammered on Nelly's front door. She opened up calmly, still wiping crumbs from the corners of her mouth with her apron.

'You're early,' she said.

'Not much,' he panted.

She hadn't even got the paint out. Brett marched into the kitchen and found Grumpus staring miserably at a funeral cutting on the table in between the dirty plate and cup and saucer. Brett was used to seeing the occasional funeral cutting grow yellow and brittle on the kitchen window-sill in his gran's house. Nelly's was clean and fresh and sat beside a fat red notebook, a pair of scissors and a PrittStick.

Nelly came in behind him, picked up the cutting, glued it into the red notebook and smoothed it down. As soon as she let go, the notebook's pages fanned open sending a breath of wind up his arm. Yuck! No wonder Grumpus looked so serious. His and Nelly's friends must all have died. Grudgingly he'd decided to forgive her for keeping him waiting, when Nelly turned round, took one look at his face and smiled.

'It's all right,' she said. 'These aren't people I know. I just collect them.'

'You collect things about people's funerals!' said Brett in a voice that echoed disgustedly round the room.

'Only certain ones,' Nelly said.

'Which ones?' demanded Brett.

'Interesting ones,' she said slyly.

Brett snorted. There wouldn't be any interesting ones. Those cuttings were creepy and horrible. His head sank in between his shoulders.

'Like this one,' said Nelly smoothing down the latest cutting and pushing the book towards him.

Brett shoved his hands in his jeans pockets and scowled at the wrinkled page. He hadn't come to read about dead bodies. Dead bodies were just for old women. He made his eyes go blurry.

'They're like Fabergé eggs,' Nelly said. 'It's like having a door opened and peeping through at someone.'

Brett's head jerked up.

'Someone dead!' he burst out. 'Yuck!'

'They're alive enough on paper,' said Nelly the elephant.

She was waiting for him to read. Brett let his eyes rest briefly on the print like two nervous flies and then hop away.

Nelly reached for the book. She was going to read it to him!

'Saturday night,' she read in a breathy voice. Brett ground his teeth to drown out as many words as he could. 'Late bus . . . Ben Jones . . . large as life. Marvellous storyteller . . . held audience spellbound like a bard of long ago . . . never more so than after a night in town. On Sunday morning he was missing from chapel. He never missed . . . scrubbed and sober in his best suit. A knot of neighbours gathered outside the end-of-terrace house. They didn't need the closed curtains to tell them that the last story had been told. The last slate miner in Tregunnor had gone.'

Was that it? Brett sniffed and peeped up at her. Now that she'd read the stupid thing, couldn't they get on with the painting? He didn't feel he could trust himself to talk about the golden egg any more, not with her rattling on about dead bodies.

'My father was a slate miner,' Nelly said.

She pointed at the photo in the oval frame where the three faces swam against a patchy background. The middle face belonged to a man. He looked dead miserable, not at all like the man in the paper who sounded like Jampot Parry in the village who got rolling drunk on a Saturday night then turned up sober as a judge in chapel on Sunday morning.

'Doesn't it make you feel you know the man?' said Nelly.

Brett shrugged to show he didn't want to know, but Nelly wouldn't let up.

'It's because he lived on his own, you see,' she said eagerly. 'If he'd had a wife and children, no one would have dared write a word about him being drunk.'

'No!' Brett gave a snuffle of agreement. 'I can just imagine what Mrs Jampot would say if . . . ' He stopped. Nelly was eyeing him with too much interest.

'Exactly,' she said. 'No one would have written about Mr Parry singing hymns on the bridge in the middle of the night. They'd have written something boring and respectable instead.' She closed the book and flicked off a crumb with a stiff finger. 'Now,' she said without looking up, 'if they were writing about you . . . '

'Ugh!' protested Brett.

'Because you've got a mother and brothers, they wouldn't mention broad beans.'

Brett's scalp prickled. He stared at Nelly with the blood rushing to his cheeks.

'But if it was a silly old cuckoo like me with no close family,' said Nelly the elephant, 'they'd say "Willows Morris . . . " Willows, that's my name.' Her face quivered.

'Willows!' scoffed Brett.

'Called after an airship built by a man called J.T. Willows,' said Nelly. 'Anyway, they'd say, if I were you that is, "Willows Morris was a person full of surprises. If you needed a painter, there was no one like her. But if you had broad beans in your garden – look out!"'

Nelly giggled. Brett's face twisted.

'Why did you ask me to paint, if you knew about the broad beans?' he cried furiously. The table moved beneath the pressure of his body and she warded it off.

'The broad bean incident is just one part of you, painting is another,' she said. 'And anyway time is running out, if I want to get things done.'

Brett stared at her. She was just a silly old woman after all, who was worried about being dead and wanted company. That's what it had all been about. The egg thing was a con. He'd quarrelled with Mark for just a load of cobblers.

And Mark would never let him forget it.

Brett was on the floor slapping the paint on the skirting when something tall and vicious crept across his lemon ceiling. It reached towards the front room door and whipped back. Brett leapt up and saw the rear wheel of Mark's bike go past the gate.

He backed into the corner and listened for the whisper of the wheels returning. First came a shadow slashing at him and cutting him down to size, then a broad bean gliding tall above the level of the hedge.

Nelly creaked towards the front door.

'Don't go out!' snapped Brett.

Nelly came back and stood in the doorway. The broad bean shadow whipped over her face. Brett put down his brush on top of the tin and nursed his throbbing finger.

'Are you packing up?' asked Nelly in a crackly voice.

'Yeah.' He wouldn't have said so, if she hadn't jumped the gun. He'd only done the skirting. It was her fault anyway for messing things up. 'I can come in the morning,' he added sullenly. 'I'll finish it then.' Once the painting was finished, she couldn't blame him for anything.

'It's Saturday,' Nelly said. 'I go to town at half past ten.'

'Ninish.'

After a pause she nodded. Her dress and shoes gave out wary rustles and creaks. Brett carried the tin to the kitchen, hammered the lid back on and dunked the brush.

'Okay,' he said brusquely.

She followed him to the front door, but he was already running through the gate and he didn't look back.

As soon as he turned breathless into his own street, Brett saw Mark's bike on the front lawn with the broad bean plant sellotaped to the frame. Brett leapt on it savagely and wrenched it off. Too late he saw Mark's dad's feet poke out from beneath his rusting car.

'What're you doing?' Len Bates's squashed face appeared between car and road.

'Getting the broad bean.'

Len Bates pushed himself out and stared at the plant as if it had dropped from a spaceship. The Bateses' garden was just a scruffy patch of grass. Len preferred engines to gardens. He was a wizard with cars, Mark said, but Mark's car didn't look as if a wizard had been anywhere near it, only a car-munching monster with rusty pawmarks. Mark's dad blew bits of rust off his face.

'You're a mad pair, you are,' he said staring greedily at the paint on Brett's jeans.

Brett scowled. He wasn't mad, everyone else was. Mark was grinning at the upstairs window. Brett pretended he hadn't seen him and stalked off with the bean.

'HEY!'

He only got as far as next door's garage. Ted was standing there with Ainsleigh, his eyes popping out of his head.

'That's Miss Morris's bean!' he blustered.

Ainsleigh jumped. Ainsleigh wasn't a fool. He'd seen the bean on Mark's bike and knew Mark would get pulped if Len Bates got to hear the full story. That's why no one ever ratted on Mark – because of his dad. Ainsleigh grabbed Ted's arm and nearly got jerked off his feet as Ted's boots hammered across the garage floor. Jean heard them and came flying out of the house, all nose and ears.

'Ted!' she said.

The moment Ted turned, Brett scarpered. Down the road he ran leaping over the front hedge, crushing the bean into a concertina. He flung it into the bin and dived into the kitchen, where Mam stood like the Statue of Liberty with a plug and screwdriver in her hand.

'Thirsty!' Brett leapt towards the sink before she started asking questions. His sticky hands closed round a mug and turned the tap on.

Steve came padding to the door. It was too quiet. Glancing round, Brett saw him and Mam exchange glances.

'What's the matter?' he demanded.

'Nothing,' Mam said mildly.

When he'd washed his hands and was heading out through the door, Mam said: 'You're back early.

Finished your painting then?'

'Nearly.' He flashed a suspicious glance at her.

'Good,' said Mam.

She thought he was fed up. She thought he was chickening out. She didn't know the half of it.

Chapter 14

Brett heard Darren get up to catch the Saturday morning bus. Steve was snoring with his mouth wide open. Brett plucked the egg book from beneath the bed and retreated under the duvet, where the twilight made skeletons of the golden eggs.

As soon as Darren had gone out of the front door, he wormed his way out of the bed, gathered up his clothes and took them downstairs.

'Brett!'

Mam wasn't really calling him. She was half asleep. He waited for her to settle, crept to the kitchen and got dressed in the corner by the broom cupboard. He made himself a piece of toast and waited till ten to nine before slipping through the hedge. The air still had a nip in it like milk ten minutes out of the fridge. Mark would still be in bed.

Nelly came to the door in men's slippers. The sleeves of her blue flecked dress hung baggy and unbuttoned and a rat's tail of hair slipped and slithered down her back. It was as if she were coming loose at the seams.

'Cup of tea?' she asked. Dark brown tea swilled round in the white china cup on the table. Its smell made Brett sick.

'Better get the painting done,' he said. 'Mam and me go to see my gran on Saturday afternoons.'

He followed the elephant out of the back door. While she unlocked the woodshed he cleared up, kicking chippings into the lumpy grass and scuffing their residue of grey powder into the cement.

He took the paint from Nelly, never lifting his eyes higher than the rat's tail of hair that snaked over her shoulder. She was ancient, horribly ancient. She always had been. He shut himself and the paint into the front room, so she wouldn't butt in on him. He had the back of the door to do, and the window-sill, then he'd have finished. Mam would say he was chickening out, but Mam was wrong. All he'd promised to do was the painting and he'd done a good job. He hadn't bargained for the spotted wallpaper, the thin brown carpet with sprays of faded orange flowers and the black sweaty chairs spoiling it all. It wasn't his fault. He couldn't be blamed for that.

He carefully brushed on the last dab of paint, snatched open the door and found Nelly standing at the kitchen window winding her hair into a knot. The dishes were washed. He put the paint tin on the clean draining board.

'Finished,' he said.

She took his word for it. 'Will you come this afternoon for your money?' she mumbled turning to him with a mouth full of pins. 'I haven't any change.'

'I'm going to my gran's.'

'Tomorrow morning before quarter to ten?'

'Yeah.'

He stared at her back. When she didn't speak, he said savagely:

'It doesn't look like an egg.'

'Pardon?' She dropped the pins into her hand.

'It doesn't look like an egg!' he repeated. He didn't want her to blame him for failing.

Nelly's bun sprang loose and hung in a bobble down the back of her neck. She turned awkwardly and creaked all the way to the front room, where the first thing she did was to grab the door and make smudge marks in the paint. She blocked the doorway.

'Painting's not enough,' said Brett. He could hear the whine in his voice and it wouldn't go away however hard he tried to sound normal. 'You've got to get wallpaper and things. You've got to find someone to paper for you.'

Nelly rubbed her fingers slowly, leaving streaks of cream pearl on her palm.

'It's like things you see in magazines,' she said sheepishly. 'Fancy cakes and fancy ideas. They're easier read than done.'

'Then you shouldn't have bothered to start,' snapped Brett.

Her eyes blinked at him in the mirror.

'It's daft!' he cried. 'If you leave it like this, it won't keep the village children away. And,' he added hurriedly, because it had sounded too much like a threat, 'they won't be able to put in the paper, "Miss Willows Morris was a quiet sort of person, but when it came to eggs – look out!"'

In response to the last bit Nelly gave one of her forgotten chuckles, but she made no promises. On his way out he slammed the door so hard he heard the egg-stone rattle.

All day Brett felt jumpy as a dog who'd lost a bone. Mam kept on looking at him as if she were in two minds whether to leave him on his own on a Saturday night.

'Brett?' she said.

'Yeah?' he growled.

'You okay?'

'Yeah!'

He was waiting for her and Steve to go. That was the best time, when they'd cleared off and the house was dead quiet. The first five minutes were especially good. It felt as if the house had been swept clean by a whirlwind. He leaned against the window and waited for the whirlwind to blow over.

As soon as his nose touched the glass, it bounced

back again. Ted Morgan was heading for the Evanses' house with a fat floppy lettuce in his hand. He had a smug look on his face, as if he was laughing up his kilt at the state of Nelly's front room. Brett dropped down on his bed. Steve was already in the car and banging the door. Mam was rushing round her room gathering up things and cursing to herself. She ran downstairs and keys rattled.

'Brett!'

Brett jumped.

'Brett?'

'Yeah?' He went to the top of the stairs.

'Okay?' said Mam.

'Yeah.'

''Bye then.'

The car jumped back into the road. Brett listened to it whine away round the estate. Silence. Only it was a prickly silence. Ted Morgan had made it prickly. It was a creepy silence too because Mark wasn't there. Mark always came round on a Saturday night.

Brett padded downstairs. The silence was thick as glass. He didn't dare put on the telly in case the noise made it shatter around him. In the end he went out to the garage. He could paint the planters for Mam with Ainsleigh's puky paints, round the back where no one could see him. But Mam had gone and shifted the paints. He nosed around a bit, but when he couldn't find them he slunk back into the house.

Ted Morgan was coming out of the Evanses' house. Brett dodged back behind the curtain as if Ted was going to throw something at him.

When he was sure that Ted had gone, Brett crept back upstairs and sat irritably cross-legged below the level of the window-sill. Beneath his bed the useless egg book shone in a droplet of evening sun. He aimed a kick at it. He may as well give it back. The sooner he forgot about eggs, the sooner things would get back to normal. He put the book in a plastic bag, but it wasn't just the book. He had to find a way of giving Nelly back too.

It was the first time Brett had ever done his homework on a Saturday night. He got out his English book and wrote without stopping about paint and bears and a funny old woman who had this thing about golden eggs. The words splattered out on the page more easily than ever before. Because the homework had to be about painting, he called it: *Death of a Painting Lady.*

Chapter 15

In the early hours of the morning Brett shot out of bed and stumbled to his mother's room.

'Mam!'

Last night's dress slid off the chair and ended up in a filmy pool on the floor. Mam lay sprawled across the middle of the double bed. He gripped her warm shoulder.

'Mam!'

'What's wrong?' She sat bolt upright.

'Where are Ainsleigh's paint tins?'

'Ainsleigh's . . . ' Mam forced her eyes open, pushed her hands through her hair.

'Where are Ainsleigh's paint tins?' Brett persisted.

'How the heck should I know?' Mam said thickly, groping for the alarm clock. She cupped her hands round it. 'It isn't half past five yet, Brett!' she screeched. 'It's . . . '

'Ainsleigh's paint tins, Mam.'

'BRETT!' roared Mam.

He fled from her into Darren's room, where he'd heard the light click on. Darren was lying on his back in his new crisp navy-blue pyjamas, blinking at him.

'What d'you want?'

'Did you move Ainsleigh's paint tins?' Brett asked, trembling.

'God!' Darren groaned and closed his eyes.

'The ones in the gar . . . '

'No, I didn't! What's the matter with you? You sound as if you've had a nightmare. For God's sake go back to bed.'

Brett retreated. There was no point asking Steve. Steve would never move anything of his own accord, not even his own stinking shoes. Anyway Steve was snoring and dangerous to touch.

Brett dropped back under the duvet. His feet were cold, but his body was too stiff to shiver. Something was wrong. He lay awkwardly like a man buried alive in a peat bog till he heard Wendy Evans across the road come back from night duty at the hospital.

It was gone half past eight. Steve was flat out. Brett slid into his clothes and crept downstairs. The back door clicked loud enough to waken the dead, but before anyone could start shouting at him, Brett dashed round the side of the house. Mam didn't bother to put the car away and never locked the garage door. But who'd steal two paint tins? Who'd be that mad?

Ainsleigh?

Maybe he'd borrowed them back to finish off some job. Brett crept up the road, but Ainsleigh's garage doors were shut. In his nightmare the paint tins had got mixed up with a dead Nelly. He had to find them.

The Evanses' cat was sitting at Ainsleigh's painted fence twitching its ears at the fish in the pond. With a silent meow it padded over and rubbed itself against Brett's legs. Brett, who was trying to open the garage door by eye power, saw Jean in her nightie look down at him from the upstairs window. He turned at once and went back to the house.

He was sitting bent double like an old man on the back doorstep and feeding the cat on scraps of cheese, when he heard the church bells ring. Ainsleigh'd be getting his car out ready for chapel. Brett lifted the cat off his lap. He was sneaking back up to Ainsleigh's, when Jean's voice cut the ground from under his feet. She'd been lying in wait.

'What are you doing then, Brett?' she called triumphantly from the open window of the front room.

Brett jumped. The cat, who had followed him, jumped in sympathy. Jean stood there framed in her spotless white blouse.

'Well?' she said.

'Nothing,' mumbled Brett.

Anyone who could look like a model in a shop window on a Sunday morning wouldn't nick two tins of paint. Ainsleigh wouldn't either. He'd have asked first, or he'd have left a note.

'Nothing,' he said picking up the cat and shuffling on up the road just for somewhere to go. The cat felt the vibrations in his body and pressed its claws in his arm. Brett took it to the playground and let it go. It landed lightly, tail swishing, on the rubber tiles and froze with arched back, its nose pointing towards Nelly's house.

'BRETT JONES!'

At once Brett's flesh moved inside his skin like icing in a bag. The roar that had burst around him came from the direction of Nelly's house.

'BRETT JONES!'

His weight dropped to his feet and anchored him to the ground. Footsteps were hammering closer and closer along the road towards him. The thin privet hedge shook. Through it plunged thick groping fingers followed by the rest of Ted Morgan in his Sunday suit.

The cat fled.

'You . . . vandal!'

Ted Morgan's hands clamped round Brett's neck and arm. Brett staggered forward and was hauled willy-nilly through the clawing hedge, past shocked faces in car windows, along the road towards Nelly's house.

'You vandal!'

They'd reached Nelly's gate. Ted thrust Brett against it and pushed his head down towards a mass of dancing pink and yellow blobs. His nightmare was coming true. Brett shied away. The missing paint had turned into a row of pink and yellow footprints that marched up the path to the front door where Nelly stood in her grey Sunday coat with a golden flower spilling off her lapel. At least she was alive.

'This is Brett's paint. He's the one who messed up your path. Ainsleigh gave him pink and yellow paint. He told me!' panted Ted.

Brett's head fell against the curved top of the gate, as Ted started pumping his back.

'He's got pink and yellow paint,' Ted spat out with each push. 'Pink and yellow.'

A bruisy pain flashed across Brett's chest. Nelly's feet were coming towards him. Nelly had grown to enormous size in her loose Sunday coat. He smelled a smell of dead flowers. Ted stopped his pumping. He pulled Brett's head back and forced him to look into Nelly's face. Someone had pulled a drawstring round her mouth.

Before Brett could manage a word, Nelly's chin dropped on her chest.

'I've seen the paint!' blasted Ted. His fingers gouged into Brett's shoulders, pulping the flesh against the bone. 'I'm going to tell your mam . . . '

'He's got yesterday's paint on his hands,' broke in Nelly in a flat voice.

'Uh?' Ted blew like a horse.

'Yesterday's paint on his hands,' murmured Nelly as if Brett wasn't there. 'Cream pearl.'

'Cream pearl?'

'Not pink or yellow.'

'He could have washed it off or something,' Ted said irritably. 'He's got the paint. I've seen it.'

'I didn't do it,' Brett choked.

'I'll see to it.' Nelly still wasn't talking to him. 'I won't come with you to chapel this morning, Ted, if you don't mind,' she said tiredly.

Ted minded. He looked ready to burst out of his Sunday suit. He let go of Brett with a gasp of disgust.

'It's getting late,' Nelly said.

A great jet of air exploded out of Ted, then he was gone. His feet screwed round on the path. In a moment his car was leaping away spitting chippings at Brett's legs. Nelly turned too. The leather of her Sunday shoes strained into creases as she followed the ugly footsteps to her own front door. Brett ran after her. He wanted to explain, but when she reached the house, she carried on up the stairs where he couldn't follow.

'I don't want it!' he cried hoarsely, as soon as he saw her reappear on the landing with the fiver in her hand. 'I don't want it!' Nelly was holding out the fiver. She wasn't interested in talking. She just wanted to pay him off and get rid of him.

'I don't want it!'

Before she'd reached the foot of the stairs, he was running down the path. He bolted along the road through the playground, through the estate, past Mark's house and didn't stop till he got to his own garage where he threw himself on the floor.

When he lifted his head, he saw his own eyes reflected back at him from the smudged sides of two tins of paint.

Chapter 16

They were Ainsleigh's tins all right, vomiting unmistakable dribbles of pink and yellow. Through the garage wall Brett heard the sudden rattle of crockery in the kitchen. He jumped to his feet, grabbed his bike and fled before Mam could see him.

Brett rode furiously through the estate, through the village, down the lane, across the blackened field. He rode straight into the river with water jetting through the wheel spokes. He didn't stop till he got to midstream where the wheels sank. He sank with them, smaller and smaller. When his one foot splashed into the water he got off his bike and jerked it to the river's edge. Brett fell down panting beside it on the wet gravel.

He closed his eyes and let the sun burn into the back

of his head till he couldn't stand it any more and rolled over.

Brett stared up at the sky. The sky burned and his eyes watered. He let the tears roll down his cheeks. It was Mark who'd done it, but he couldn't tell Nelly that. No one ever ratted on Mark because of his dad.

Brett sat up and cradled his head on his knees. It wasn't his fault. His trainers were steaming and on the gravel his footprints were drying to a milky grey. He stared down at the white stones. It wasn't fair. He could stay here for ever and ever and those other footprints wouldn't go away.

At least he could get rid of the paint on his hands. He scratched furiously at the arcs of white around his nails, at the pools that gathered between his fingers and the trickles that followed the lines of his palms. On his left palm he uncovered the yellow dot he'd left there as an ejector button that day in Ainsleigh's garage. Fat lot of good it had done him. He scratched at it and didn't stop scratching till his hand felt raw.

The pain made him angrier. He picked up a stone and flung it across the gravel.

'Swine, Mark!' he screamed.

The stone bounced off the field edge and landed on a pale green leaf.

Brett turned round. More and more pale green leaves were pushing through the burnt earth. To a bird flying overhead they'd look like green stars in a velvet sky. Soon they'd cover the black completely.

The spot on the palm of Brett's hand throbbed. His

head dropped on his knees and he sat for minutes on end wrapped up in himself till a thought began to take shape inside him. First it was elusive as mist. Then he caught it and let it incubate and grow into something real. When at last he was sure he could do it, he got to his feet and carried it carefully up the hill to his own kitchen door.

Mam was enjoying a cup of coffee.

'Mam!'

She heard the quietness in his voice and stared.

'Will you take me to town this afternoon, if I clean the car for you?'

Mam's eyebrows rose. 'Oh, yeah?'

'Please.'

'What for?'

'To buy paint.'

'Brett Jones!' she sighed.

'Please!'

'Okay,' she said. 'Put it like that and I will.'

He got a tin of grey paint with the first fiver Nelly'd given him and some money of his own. It looked the right sort of paint. The tin was wedged between his feet when they got back to Greenhill and Len Bates lumbered out of the playground. Mam slammed on her brakes.

'That man wastes all his money on drink,' she cried. 'No wonder Mark . . . ' She broke off and set her lips in a thin line.

Brett wasn't thinking of Mark. Mark had become

someone hard and distant, separated from him by a pink and yellow line. He wasn't thinking of anything. He was waiting.

He waited till a quarter to six, the time when Ted and Mrs Ted picked up Nelly for the evening service. As soon as 5.45 had flashed on his digital watch, Brett let the handle of the tin slide into the grooves of his fingers. He picked up the paintbrush and walked through the hedge as though the hedge wasn't there. He walked along the main road, up Nelly's path and knocked on the front door just in case.

A sigh ran through the walls of the house like a breath of wind blowing through the cracks. He knocked again and this time the house was silent.

Swiftly Brett walked back to the gate, hung a warning exclamation over the post and dropped on his knees out of sight. It was simple, his plan. He was going to paint the footprints away. He'd done it with Mark and he could do it with the paint.

The hedge gave him shelter from passing cars. He took a screwdriver from his pocket and loosened the lid of the tin. He plunged the brush into the coarse grey paint and with it attacked the pink and yellow footprints. They were bigger than his own and hopped pigeon-toed and slowly fading towards Nelly's front door. He buried them under a layer of paint so thick that the holes in the concrete bubbled and rivulets trickled into the grass on each side.

The paint unwound behind him in a grey matt carpet. When he reached the step, the house gave what sounded like a sigh of approval. Brett stopped just long enough to glance at the black windows above his head, then retreated, painting a second coat faster and faster. He chased every last scrap of paint round the sides of the tin and plastered in onto the path.

Once the painting was done, he fell back onto the grass. His arms were vibrating, his fingers tingling and his knees were sore. A spot of blood seeped through the paint on his middle finger, but he felt good.

He'd done it. He looked around him. Yes, he'd done it. Nelly's path was as good as new. Better! Just as long as Nelly stepped from the roadside onto the grass.

He jumped to his feet, went out through the gate and tried stepping over the path. It was easy. He could just imagine Nelly giving one of her rusty chuckles when she saw it. Everything would be okay. Pity he wouldn't be there to see her face. He gave the gate a triumphant rub with an old T-shirt where he'd left sticky marks, and threw the T-shirt in the air.

The sun chose that very moment to polish up his other paintwork in the front room. It glimmered so like the pictures in Nelly's book that he jumped over the paint and ran to press his face against the window.

When he saw inside the room, he felt a shock that welded him to the glass. He tore himself away and fled with a cry of pain down the garden path.

Chapter 17

Brett ran in slow motion through the gate and down the road. He didn't see Ted Morgan's car glide up nor hear the shout behind him. He didn't feel a thing till a hand swung him savagely round and a voice screamed, 'Caught you this time!' in his face.

Ted Morgan had him by the collar and Greenhill on a summer evening was swaying round him in a sea of blood-red sparks. He clawed at Ted's hands.

'I caught you redhanded this time!' spluttered Ted. 'You've done the path again! You thought we were in chapel, didn't you? But I knew you'd come back. I knew!'

'She's dead!' Brett gasped. A great sob rose inside him as soon as he heard himself speak. 'Nel . . . Miss Morris is lying on the floor of the front room. I've just seen her. She's dead.'

Ted let go as if Brett had bitten him. Slowly he turned.

'What have you done?' he whispered. 'What have you DONE?'

He began to move towards Nelly's house cautiously, then faster and faster he ran leaving behind him a line of pale grey footsteps. Brett followed with an ache in his side that pulled the top half of his body forward. He crashed against the gate. The grey paint was a cheesy mess that overspilled across the grass to the front window where Ted stood.

A whimper came from Ted's throat. He pounded down the side of the house. Brett heard the echoes from inside the house, saw the door fly open. Ted Morgan stood on the doorstep. His cheeks were blood-red, his face muscles jumping.

'Get away from here!' he spat. 'Get AWAY!'

'Miss M . . . '

'Get AW-AAAAAY!'

Brett turned. His feet were heavy as lead. Chippings mixed with paint had stuck to his soles. On cemented trainers he stumbled down the long road past the playground, past Mark's, past Ainsleigh's to his own house where he crashed against the front door. A retching sound brought Mam running to open the door and Steve leaping down the stairs.

'Brett! Bretty boy!' Mam fell on her knees with her arms around him.

'She's dead!' he cried.

'Miss Morris?'

'I saw her. She's lying on the floor of the front room.'

'Oh my God!' Mam let go and stood trembling over him. 'We've got to get an ambulance.'

'Ted Morgan's there,' choked Brett.

'Oh, poor Bretty!' Mam whispered in a cracked voice. She had grey paint on her sleeve where she'd touched him. 'Poor Bretty boy!'

'He's daft!' Steve was shaking. 'What did he want to go painting for? He's only a kid.'

'I'll go over,' Mam said.

She stepped out in her old slippers leaving Brett groping for the banister rails.

'Brett!' Steve's sharp angry voice broke over his head as soon as Mam had gone. 'You haven't been doing anything?'

'No-oooo!' wailed Brett. 'Don't be stupid!'

Steve went into the front room. Brett could hear him at the window. He was trying not to think. He was trying to stop his mind. By the time he heard Mam's footsteps running back along the road he felt empty inside, his skin the skin of a long-dead animal, dry and cracking. Mam was shouting at him before she'd even crossed the lawn.

'Miss Morris has been attacked!' she cried. 'Someone's mugged her.'

Brett saw her gather up a fallen slipper and run barefoot into the house. He lifted his face.

'I thought she'd had a stroke or something,' Mam wailed. 'Why didn't you tell me? Why didn't you tell me?' She shook him and went on shaking even after he'd told her that he hadn't known.

'She was still alive when the ambulance came,' whispered Mam.

Grey paint had splattered down the back of Mam's legs. It was there in the hallway, mottling the carpet. She sank down in front of Brett and slid an arm round his waist.

'Brett,' she whispered, brushing the hair from his eyes, 'you've got to tell me if it's your fault.'

'It's the painting's fault!' Brett snapped, pulling himself away from her.

'Oh my God!' Her voice came wailing after him up the stairs.

She'd changed into her green suit by the time the policemen came, the one she bought for Aunty Joy's wedding with the wine stain on the sleeve. She'd made him change too and scrub the paint off his hands and hair. His hair was still wet when the ring came at the door.

Mam sat on the edge of the settee with her long legs between him and the policemen.

'He's had a shock,' she said.

The policemen didn't care about shocks. The one who spoke had a soft voice and a smile that slid like shadows into the crevices of his face. But he asked Brett about Nelly's money that had been stolen from upstairs. And he made him talk about the pink and yellow footprints.

When she heard about the footprints, Mam's knees started trembling beneath the green skirt.

'I didn't put the footprints there, Mam,' he whispered, pressing the tip of his finger into her side.

'Who did?' asked the policemen politely, as if they didn't believe him.

'Don't know.'

Mam turned to look at him.

'Don't know!' he repeated.

No one ever ratted on Mark because of his dad. He couldn't do it. It wasn't the path that mattered anyway.

Chapter 18

'Brett.' Cannon stood over him as he gathered in the English books during registration. 'Are you all right?'

'Sir.'

Mam had said he'd feel better if he went to school, but he didn't. His mouth was dry and his insides like a lump of lead. The seat beside him was empty. Mark wasn't in school. He hadn't come on the bus.

From the school yard at break-time he saw the hospital windows flash on the other side of town. Nelly was in the hospital. He could only picture her curled up like a hedgehog that a dog had been plaguing. A police car slid in at the school gate and parked with barely a whisper beside the Head's office.

During break-time Winffie and Tim had been telling 7B what had happened, so that when Cannon appeared at the door during the maths lesson, everyone knew he'd come for Brett. Anne James, the maths teacher, turned round to find all eyes watching Cannon and Cannon watching Brett.

Cannon's voice was hardly above a whisper.

'May I borrow Brett Jones?'

'You may.' Anne James chuckled. Brett was the sort of boy you could easily spare from a maths lesson.

Brett knocked against Davina's chair. He felt Cannon's hand on his shoulders kneading, kneading. Cannon steered him down the stairs, along the corridor. It was only when they were within sight of the Headmaster's study that Cannon's grip tightened and brought him to a halt against the wall.

'Brett,' he whispered in a hoarse voice. 'You know your homework?'

Brett's mouth opened.

'It's about Miss Morris, isn't it?'

At the sound of her name, Brett's heart began to echo like a plunger inside him. He'd forgotten about the homework.

'Is it about Miss Morris?' persisted Cannon.

'Yeah.' The blood began to prickle in Brett's cheeks. He felt as if a soft cool wave washed over him. 'Yeah!' His eyes brightened. He'd done something right after all. He'd actually done it. Even if Nelly died, people would know about her, because he'd written about her just like the people in the red book. Perhaps that's what she'd always wanted him to do.

At the far end of the corridor the door of the

Headmaster's study opened. Brett saw the two policemen of the night before sitting at the far end of the desk with their heads bent over an exercise book. They were reading about Nelly.

'Don't worry, Brett,' whispered Cannon, but Brett was too busy sorting the words out in his head.

'Miss Morris has died.' It was something like that he'd written. 'She was the old lady who lived in the grey house with a bear called Grumpus. You most probably thought she was a mean old bag. She was always shouting at kids and spying. But perhaps it was the kids' fault, or perhaps she was lonely. Anyway, because her fingers were stiff she couldn't do what she wanted.'

Cannon's fingers made him move, but still the words kept on running like a tape round Brett's head. They sounded right. Nelly would like them.

'She wanted to make a golden egg! – like the ones the tsars made for their friends in Russia. She wanted to make her front room into a golden egg, so when you looked in through the window it would be a surprise. So she got an understanding person to paint for her and she bought some cream pearl and white with a hint of lemon paint.

'It was brill to start off with, but it wasn't enough.

'You had to have furniture and carpets and wallpaper to make a golden egg.

'So the egg could never be finished and when her painter left, she died.'

The Headmaster was making way for him. The

smiling policeman raised his eyes.

'Hello, Brett.'

Brett stared. The tape was still running in his head.

'What does this say, Brett?'

The book slid towards him across the table. Cannon hadn't marked it. For once there were no words neatly printed in red in the margin, only his own, black and spiky, sprawled across the page. His words always came out blacker than everyone else's, even though he used the same sort of biro as Mark.

'Death of a Painting Lady,' Brett said promptly.

'Death . . . of a Painting Lady,' repeated the policeman. 'When did you write it, Brett?'

'Saturday night.'

'Saturday night?' queried the policeman.

Brett felt the tremble of Cannon's fingers on his sleeve.

'Sat . . . urday night,' repeated the policeman. 'Not Sunday?'

Brett shuddered. Sunday was last night. He couldn't have written it Sunday.

'Why did you do it, Brett?'

It was quiet in the room. Brett heard the echo of his words like pebbles in a pool.

'Because she wanted me to.'

'To do what, Brett?' asked the policeman softly.

'To write an . . . ' The word had gone out of his head.

'Obituary?'

'Yeah.' Brett smiled.

The smile was lost on the men around him. They were watching him with wary thoughtful eyes. Cannon's hand vibrated on his shoulder.

'She wanted me to,' Brett said stoutly.

The policeman stared at the words on the page. He wasn't even looking at Brett, when he asked in a crisp voice, 'How did you know that she was going to be attacked on Sunday then, Brett?' When Brett didn't answer, he fixed him with a look that was no longer smiling. 'How did you know that, Brett?'

'I didn't.' What was the policeman on about? Brett looked up at Cannon. Cannon's craggy face had gone soft as putty. Wrinkles formed and reformed at the corners of his eyes.

'You didn't know she was going to be attacked on the Sunday?' the policeman persisted.

'No!'

'Then why . . . ?'

'Because she wanted me to,' cried Brett. Was the man trying to say he'd attacked Nelly? It was daft. He wouldn't have written about her like that, if he'd wanted to do her in. 'She wanted me to. Well . . . ' He shook his head furiously. Nelly hadn't actually asked, but she'd have wanted him to write. That's why she'd shown him the funeral cuttings. He turned to Cannon. 'Nell . . . Miss Morris collected thingies . . . funeral thingies.'

'Obituaries?'

'Yeah! She collected them, when they were interesting, about people who lived on their own. I didn't think she was going to die . . . '

'She's not going to die, Brett,' said Cannon huskily.

'I just did it because I was in the mood and before I could forget, because I was the only one who knew about the egg.' Brett turned to the policemen. 'The egg!' he said.

They replied with a blank look.

'It's in the book!' Brett cried.

The two men stared at the book. Slowly the smiling policeman turned the page.

'I'd been painting for her,' Brett explained in a panic. 'She wanted me to make her front room like the inside of a golden egg. It says so.'

The policemen exchanged glances.

They hadn't read it. They couldn't even read it now. His words weren't like anyone else's words. People were always telling him his letters got jumbled up. He hadn't written about Nelly at all. All he'd written was rubbish.

He *was* rubbish. All he'd done for Nelly was draw Mark's attention to her. It was Condor's field all over again.

Chapter 19

The rest of 7B looked at Brett curiously as he returned whitefaced to his desk. As soon as the bell went for lunch break, he snatched his bag and threaded his way to the school gates.

'Brett!'

Steve's voice couldn't stop him. There were just five minutes to go before the twelve-ten bus left for St.Hermon and he got there with seconds to spare.

By the time the bus dropped him at the stop just past Greenhill, Brett had been up to Mark's house more than a dozen times. He'd got Mark out of hiding. He'd made Mark go to the police to confess. Mark couldn't be allowed to get away with hurting Nelly, any more than he could get away with Condor's field.

He climbed over the side hedge into Greenhill and

saw a white face peep out of the bedroom window opposite his house. Wendy Evans wasn't asleep even though she'd been on night duty. The estate was dead quiet and holding its breath.

Brett threw his school bag into the garage and without stopping carried on up the road to Mark's. When he was just by Ainsleigh's, he saw a movement inside the house. At once he darted across the lawn and pressed his finger hard on the doorbell.

No answer. The car wasn't there. Mark's mam worked odd hours in the old people's home. Brett slipped round the side. Through the window he saw the kitchen table littered with empty beer cans. Quietly he tried the handle of the kitchen door, but the door was locked.

'Mark!' he hissed.

Brett put his ear to the glass pane. Someone was in the house all right. He could hear a creaky breath. Brett dropped down on all fours, crept past the front window and pounced on the letterbox. Through the flap he saw Len Bates's face fly at him, the colour of rotten meat. Before he could let go, the door opened dragging him inside and flinging him to the floor.

'What the hell d'you think you're doing?' Len Bates ground through his teeth.

'Looking for Mark,' Brett stammered.

He grasped at the banister and pulled himself up. Len Bates came up close with his sick beery breath. Len drew the air back in till his chest bulged over his belt.

'Mark,' he said thickly. 'Isn't he in school?'

'School?' The word came out in a bleat. No one ever answered Len Bates's questions if there was a chance they'd get Mark into trouble.

Len Bates was letting air out softly through his teeth. When the very last breath had gone, he lunged suddenly. Brett ducked and Len hooked himself round the end of the banister.

'Mark!' he bellowed up the stairs. 'Mark! Maaaaark!' As his voice died away, he slumped onto the stairs and lay like a deflated balloon with his face red and ugly against the rails.

Brett listened for a noise from upstairs. He forgot about being angry with Mark. If Mark was hiding upstairs and Len Bates got to him first, there'd be nothing left of him.

'I'll go and look,' he cried thinly.

Len Bates's red face against the banister never blinked. Brett squeezed between Len and the wall. He ran up to Mark's bedroom and felt a weight against the door handle.

'Mark!' he whispered.

A sound behind him made him jump. Len Bates was on his feet, his face balanced like an egg against the bottom of the banister rails. With a grunt he launched himself up the stairs and charged along the landing at Mark's door. The door opened and snapped shut. Grunting and panting Len held it ajar and pushed Brett through the gap. Brett stumbled over a mattress that lay wedged between the gaping wardrobe and door. Mark's bedclothes and the contents of the wardrobe lay strewn across the floor. In the midst of the heap lay one of Mark's old trainers with a pink-painted sole. As Brett hesitated, Len Bates's hands clamped round his neck.

'What do you want Mark for?' he panted. 'Where is he? Why're you snooping? Why're you snooping?'

'I thought Mark was ill,' yelped Brett. He tried to twist his face away from Len's breath.

'Why're you snooping, Brett Jones? What's Mark told you, eh?'

Brett couldn't swallow. Len's hands were choking him.

'I haven't seen Mark. I thought he was ill,' he cried.

'Why should he be ill?'

'I just thought . . . '

Len Bates let him go. Brett grabbed at the window-sill and pulled himself up.

'Why should Mark be ill?' spat Len. 'What's the matter with everyone, just because of that Morris woman?'

Len knew! Brett's breath made a lump in his throat. Len Bates was trampling over Mark's duvet with his big feet. If he'd guessed about Mark and Miss Morris, then maybe Mark was already pulverised. Mark's mam too. Brett's breath came out in a squeal. He put up an arm to ward the man off.

'Miss Morris is getting better,' he cried.

Len stopped in his tracks. His eyes narrowed.

'Who says?' he snapped.

'Mr Harris in school,' Brett stammered. 'He said she could get better.'

Len Bates breathed noisily. Through the sound of his breathing came the whine of Mam's car. Brett glanced over his shoulder and saw the red Metro swerve into the street. Before it had stopped properly, she was out of it and calling his name.

'It's Mam. She's down at our house. Ah!' he gasped. Len Bates was pressing him against the window-sill. His hand locked around Brett's wrist.

'We'll get some flowers then,' he panted.

'Flowers?' whispered Brett.

'We'll take them to her.'

Len Bates dragged Brett over the duvet. His head scraped against the bedroom door. He fell on the bottom stairs and scrambled on his hands and knees with Len still dragging. His feet sent a beer can skidding across the kitchen floor. Len pushed him through the back door onto the scabby lawn edged with broken concrete where the grass grew matted and sick-looking. In next door's garden Ainsleigh's aeroplane whirred, sending wafts of flowers over the wooden fencing.

'Get over to Ainsleigh's garden.' Len grunted.

Brett whimpered.

'Bloody fool!' In two strides Len Bates had elbowed past him and was aiming a kick at the bottom planks of the fence. A second kick splintered the wood. Len pushed his hand through the gap and tore at Ainsleigh's flowers. Brett backed away, reached the side path, turned and ran. He was haring across Ainsleigh's front lawn, when he heard a grunt behind him.

'Mam!' He plunged straight through the fish pond with Len clawing at his back. He could see Mam at the front room window. 'Mam!' he screamed as the pavement flew under his wet shoes. He crashed sidelong into her car and before he could pick himself up, Len was on him. He opened the car door, pushed Brett inside and flung himself on top. The key rattled in the ignition.

'Len!'

Brett heard Mam's scream as Len started the car and swung it round onto the opposite pavement. He struggled to get his hands free and reach the door handle.

'Fool!' Len got hold of the back of his shirt, so he couldn't breathe. 'Shut it!'

Mam's wail followed the car as it seesawed past the playground.

'Where's Mark?' Brett wrenched himself free. 'Where's Mark?' he cried. 'If Mark's okay, it's better he goes to the police.'

'Police?'

Len Bates took his eyes off the road.

'Watch out!' screamed Brett.

The car bounced off the kerb. Donna James's white face filled the window above Brett's head as she snatched her baby's pushchair out of the way.

'If he's bloody told the police I done it,' Len Bates

panted, 'I'll bloody . . . '

Bloody . . . Brett struggled up. He barely saw the lorry heading towards them, barely flinched as Len swerved.

'You!' he cried and his voice went on rising as he stared at the man beside him. 'You did it!'

'Mean old bloody bitch she was anyway.'

'Is!' Brett screamed at him. 'She's not dead. And there's no point in running away. Nelly'll be able to tell the police about you.'

'She bloody won't!'

Len was shaking the wheel to make the car go faster. Petals from Ainsleigh's garden trickled down his clothes. They were petals for Nelly's funeral. Len Bates, drunken Len, was going to go to the hospital to get her.

'SHE WILL!' cried Brett. He clamped himself round the man's arm. The car mounted the verge and bounced back onto the road, just as Condor's red tractor nosed out of the farm gate. In a split second with a juddering crack tractor and road disappeared. Petals, leaves, grass, waves and waves of corn swung in a spiral and poured past Brett's window. The sky slipped sideways and Len Bates slumped hard against him with blood in his hair.

The car lay suddenly quiet on its roof. Green cornstalks pressed against the window. Brett's eyes closed. When he opened them again, a mist was blowing through the corn, the car was rocking and voices shouted. He felt Len Bates slide off and hands reached out for him.

'Don't,' he grumbled.

'Brett.'

He was far too tired to push the rough hands away. They made the car door scratch his face. They made him rattle and bump across the field. He'd turned into an aching larva that whined and whined till he was laid down on cool cow-smelling grass with Ray Condor panting over him. Brett opened his eyes. Someone had lit a fire just where the car was. He saw the corn turn red and sweep across the valley.

'Brett.'

Mam was sliding beside him in a tangle of arms and legs. The heaving of her chest made his hair turn into powder and fall across his face. He struggled to get up as her body folded over him.

'Brett,' she whispered. 'Take it easy, love.'

Brett's eyes watered in the stinging air. Someone was making a black path across the valley floor. It was burning away his eye in the cornfield.

Chapter 20

He lay still. The walls were all pale cream. No Blu-tack. Mam turned suddenly from the window.

'It's Mr Harris your form-teacher,' she said. 'Perhaps he's come to see you.'

Brett didn't move. They'd put him in a hospital room near a ward where babies were crying and little children running.

'You be nice to him now, Brett,' Mam said. 'He's been very worried about you. He's the one who phoned me to say that someone had seen you catch the bus home. If I hadn't come, God knows what that Len Bates would have done to you.'

Mam shivered. Her blonde hair stuck out in wisps around her face. She looked almost as young as Darren's girlfriend.

Brett tried to think about Darren's girlfriend, but nothing would stick in his head. In time he heard Cannon coming down the corridor, first his low voice, then the soft pad of his Size 11 shoes following the nurse's scuttling feet. For a big man Cannon walked like a cat.

Mam said, 'Mr Harris!' and Cannon came in.

'How are you, Brett?' Cannon said.

''Right, thanks,' whispered Brett, but beneath the sheets he felt small, raw, soft-boned as a baby.

He turned his head away and let Cannon talk to Mam. Then Mam went and the bed creaked. Cannon was sitting beside him.

'Brett,' said Cannon, 'I've been thinking.'

The words hurt his head. Brett listened to their reverberations without moving a muscle.

'About your Miss Morris . . . We could ask the Social Care Group in school for money . . . You could do out her room for her by the time she comes out of hospital . . . Brett?' Cannon touched his shoulder.

The thumping in Brett's head grew worse. He could feel it shaking the flesh of his cheeks.

'I can't paper!' he said abruptly.

'We'll pay people to help,' Cannon said.

Brett shook his head.

A baby gave a piercing wail in the next room. When Mark had hit his head in September, they'd put him in the men's ward.

'You can choose the paper and everything, Brett,' Cannon said. 'You're the one who knows about golden eggs like the tsars made for their friends in Russia.'

Brett turned his eyes sharply to the man's face. Where had Cannon got those words from?

'You are the understanding painter chosen by Miss Morris, aren't you – the one you mentioned in your essay?' smiled Cannon. 'Well, think about it.' He left a box of Roses on the bedside table and went before Brett could thank him.

Steve had most of the Roses. Darren was too worried about his teeth. Steve dribbled chocolate onto Brett's clean bedsheet when he was trying to tell a joke.

'Pig!' said Brett.

'You look better now after that bit of sleep,' said Mam. 'That and your brothers cheering you up.'

'He's a blinking layabout,' said Steve, giving the handle of the bed a turn.

'Leave him alone, Steve,' said Mam. 'Brett's been very brave and ver . . . ' She caught Steve pulling faces behind her back and Brett giggled.

'He's a nutter,' Steve said, helping himself to another chocolate.

Once they'd gone, Brett tried getting up. From his room he could see across the car park. Somewhere above him Mark's dad was in intensive care with a police guard round him and Nelly was getting better in another ward. She'd already told the police it was Mark's dad just before the accident, so it wasn't him that had ratted on Len Bates. Nelly had saved him that. Mark was down at his gran's but when he saw

Mark, he would tell him so.

In a flash of white socks Brett recognised his own dad tearing across the parking ground in pressed shorts. He paused by Mam like a relay racer then ran on. Brett sighed and propped himself up on his elbow.

Dad's nose came round the door first, then his floppy hair, then the rest of him, lean and bony.

'I only just heard,' he panted.

''s okay.'

'Your mam left a note – well, a huge letter actually – under the door, but I was out training.'

''s okay.'

'You okay?' asked Dad.

'Yeah,' said Brett.

'You've been painting then?' Dad flopped on the end of the bed. 'For Miss Willows Morris.'

Brett jumped. 'How did you know her name was Willows?' he demanded. 'Mam didn't.'

'Ah!' Dad tapped his nose.

Brett sat up.

'I took a photo of her once,' said Dad cheerfully. 'Her and her mam and dad.'

'You did!'

'I just fancied myself as a bit of a photographer then.'

'It wasn't a thing like a jigsaw with three faces, was it?' Brett burst out.

'Yeah!' beamed Dad. 'Did she show it to you? Arty, wasn't it? None of your common or garden photographs for me. I was all set on being a photographer then, see. I did double exposures and things. Miss Morris said she liked the photograph, bless her. I thought she just said it to humour me, but maybe she did really like it. She was a good old sport once you got to know her.'

'Still is,' said Brett, but Dad was scratching his bony ankle and checking beneath a white sock to see what damage he'd done. It was on the tip of Brett's tongue to tell him about the Fabergé egg, when a nurse poked her head in. Her eyes were drawn to the white socks like a moth to light.

'Only just heard,' said Dad, before she could ask him to leave. 'He's my son.'

'Oh?' The nurse threw a pitying glance at Brett.

Brett ignored it. So what if he did have a dad who wore white socks and Boy Scout shorts? At least his dad didn't pulverise people. At this very moment he was poking his stomach. Brett heard the sound of a zip and from a purse round his waist Dad produced a tenner and waved it at him.

'Didn't have time to buy anything. Will this do?'

'Wow!' said Brett.

'You get something for yourself.'

'Thanks!' said Brett.

'That's okay,' said Dad contentedly.

Before he went, Dad said: 'You should sleep all right here. You'll get a bit of peace in a room of your own.'

Fancy Dad knowing that. Maybe Mam was right and he did have bits of Dad in him after all. Maybe he had bits of all sorts of people stretching right back into the mists of time. He was keeping them alive like Nelly kept the people in the red book. He'd keep Nelly alive too.

Brett got out of bed to tuck the tenner in the drawer behind the soap bag Mam had brought for him. The tenner could come in handy.

Chapter 21

In the end it was Cannon who paid to redecorate Nelly's front room out of the Social Care Fund. And it was Cannon who got together the decorating team which included Ainsleigh (wall-papering), Ted, a very humble anxious-to-please Ted (dogsbody) and Jean (chair-covering and curtains). But it was Brett who chose the wallpaper with its pearly shell shapes in soft yellow with haloes of silver grey, the yellow curtains and flecked carpet to match. And it was Brett whom people consulted about the golden egg.

A weekend's work and Nelly's old front room had all but gone. It was meant to be a secret, but Brett suspected that Nelly knew as she sat confidently in her chair in the back garden of the nursing home with the local paper on her knee.

'No interesting obituaries today,' she said when she caught Brett's eyes straying stealthily over the page.

'Good,' said Brett. 'It means that no interesting people are dead. Anyway when are you coming home?'

'Next weekend?' she asked.

'Yeah,' he said. 'Fine. Okay.'

Ted had already booked the carpet men for the Friday afternoon. Once they'd gone Brett set to to paint the messed-up path. He was kneeling at the gate with his pot of paint beside him when he saw Mark's face flash by. He scrambled up and watched the brake lights of the Bateses' car disappear round Condor's corner. Ainsleigh was coming round the side of the house.

'I just saw Mark,' Brett said jerkily.

'Mark?' Ainsleigh stopped at the hedge and did one of his slow-motion raisings of the eyebrows.

'He just went past in the car. He must have been home.' Mark hadn't been home at all, not since the crash. His gran's house was sixty miles away.

'Collecting things, I expect,' mused Ainsleigh.

Brett moved closer. There was something he had to get off his chest.

'I thought it was Mark,' he confessed. 'I thought it was Mark attacked Miss Morris.'

'He's had a bad time, that boy,' was Ainsleigh's slow reply. 'You hear a lot living next door, see. But his mam's a good girl and with his dad in prison he'll have a fresh start down at his gran's.'

Brett watched him. Believing that Mark had done it had seemed almost a crime in itself, but by the look on Ainsleigh's face he didn't think it so wrong.

'Drop him a line,' said Ainsleigh suddenly.

'Eh?' said Brett.

'Write to him,' said Ainsleigh. 'Just a quick letter. Just to show you're thinking of him. He might need it.'

'Yeah,' said Brett.

He could get Steve to spell it out for him. On second thoughts he wouldn't. If he wrote it himself, it would give Mark a laugh. Mark would appreciate that. He might even bother to reply. He gave Ainsleigh a wink for thinking of it, then went back to his job of blotting out the messed-up pink and yellow footprints.

The path was ready for Nelly to walk up the very next day between Ainsleigh and Ted. Jean had set up a table lamp on just the right spot on the mantelpiece in the front room. Its light skipped from silver halo to silver halo till the whole wall shone. Even people in their cars could see it.

But Nelly's face was blank. Her legs seemed rubbery and her shoes too big for her feet. Brett slipped out of the front room and stood at the foot of the stairs. She was having difficulty getting up the steps. Ted let go of her arm and she leaned against the spindly cupboard for support. Brett had stepped forward to help her when he felt something pressed against his palm, something smooth and hard that warmed to the touch.

'Thanks!' With a grin Brett flung his arms round her waist as if he'd known her for a hundred years. In his hand was the egg-shaped stone he'd thrown into Nelly's garden so many weeks before. It was okay! Nelly was telling him he'd done it.

An egg for an egg.

Other great reads from ***Red Fox***

Further Red Fox titles that you might enjoy reading are listed on the following pages. They are available in bookshops or they can be ordered directly from us.

If you would like to order books, please send this form and the money due to:

ARROW BOOKS, BOOKSERVICE BY POST, PO BOX 29, DOUGLAS, ISLE OF MAN, BRITISH ISLES. Please enclose a cheque or postal order made out to Arrow Books Ltd for the amount due, plus 75p per book for postage and packing to a maximum of £7.50, both for orders within the UK. For customers outside the UK, please allow £1.00 per book.

NAME____

ADDRESS______________________________________

____

Please print clearly.

Whilst every effort is made to keep prices low, it is sometimes necessary to increase cover prices at short notice. If you are ordering books by post, to save delay it is advisable to phone to confirm the correct price. The number to ring is THE SALES DEPARTMENT 071 (if outside London) 973 9700.

Enter the gripping world of the REDWALL saga

REDWALL Brian Jacques

It is the start of the summer of the Late Rose. Redwall Abbey, the peaceful home of a community of mice, slumbers in the warmth of a summer afternoon.

But not for long. Cluny is coming! The evil one-eyed rat warlord is advancing with his battle-scarred mob. And Cluny wants Redwall . . .

ISBN 0 09 951200 9 £3.99

MOSSFLOWER Brian Jacques

One late autumn evening, Bella of Brockhall snuggled deep in her armchair and told a story . . .

This is the dramatic tale behind the bestselling *Redwall*. It is the gripping account of how Redwall Abbey was founded through the bravery of the legendary mouse Martin and his epic quest for Salmandastron.

ISBN 0 09 955400 3 £3.99

MATTIMEO Brian Jacques

Slagar the fox is intent on revenge . . .

On bringing death and destruction to the inhabitants of Redwall Abbey, in particular to the fearless warrior mouse Matthias. His cunning and cowardly plan is to steal the Redwall children—and Mattimeo, Matthias' son, is to be the biggest prize of all.

ISBN 0 09 967540 4 £3.99

MARIEL OF REDWALL Brian Jacques

Brian Jacques starts his second trilogy about Redwall Abbey with the adventures of the mousemaid Mariel, lost and betrayed by Slagar the Fox, but fighting back with all her spirit.

ISBN 0 09 992960 0 £4.50

Other great reads from **Red Fox**

Action-Packed Drama with Red Fox Fiction!

SIMPLE SIMON Yvonne Coppard

Simon isn't stupid – he's just not very good at practical things. So when Mum collapses, it's Cara, his younger sister who calls the ambulance and keeps a cool head. Simon plans to show what he can do too, in a crisis, but his plan goes frighteningly wrong . . .
ISBN 0 09 910531 4 £2.99

LOW TIDE William Mayne

Winner of the Guardian Children's Fiction Award.

The low tide at Jade Bay leaves fish on dry land and a wreck high on a rock. Is this the treasure ship the divers have been looking for? Three friends vow to find out – and find themselves swept away into adventure.
ISBN 0 09 918311 0 £3.50

THE INTRUDER John Rowe Townsend

It isn't often that you meet someone who claims to be you. But that's what happens to Arnold Haithwaite. The real Arnold has to confront the menacing intruder before he takes over his life completely.
ISBN 0 09 999260 4 £3.50

GUILTY Ruth Thomas

Everyone in Kate's class says that the local burglaries have been done by Desmond Locke's dad, because he's just come out of prison. Kate and Desmond think otherwise and set out to prove who really is *guilty*.
ISBN 0 09 918591 1 £2.99

Other great reads from **Red Fox**

Top teenage fiction from Red Fox

PLAY NIMROD FOR HIM Jean Ure

Christopher and Nick are each other's only friend. Isolated from the rest of the crowd, they live in their own world of writing and music. Enter lively, popular Sal who tempts Christopher away from Nick . . .
ISBN 0 09 985300 0 £2.99

HAMLET, BANANAS AND ALL THAT JAZZ
Alan Durant

Bert, Jim and their mates vow to live dangerously – just as Nietzsche said. So starts a post-GCSEs summer of girls, parties, jazz, drink, fags . . . and tragedy.
ISBN 0 09 997540 8 £3.50

ENOUGH IS TOO MUCH ALREADY
Jan Mark

Maurice, Nina and Nazzer are all re-sitting their O levels but prefer to spend their time musing over hilarious previous encounters with strangers, hamsters, wild parties and Japanese radishes . . .
ISBN 0 09 985310 8 £2.99

BAD PENNY Allan Frewin Jones

Christmas doesn't look good for Penny this year. She's veggy, feels overweight, *and* The Lizard, her horrible father has just turned up. Worse still, Roy appears – Penny's ex whom she took a year to get over.
ISBN 0 09 985280 2 £2.99

CUTTING LOOSE Carole Lloyd

Charlie's horoscope says to get back into the swing of things, but it's not easy: her Dad and Gran aren't speaking, she's just found out the truth about her mum, and is having severe confused spells about her lovelife. It's time to cut loose from all binding ties, and decide what she wants and who she really is.
ISBN 0 09 91381 X £3.50

Other great reads from ***Red Fox***

Teenage thrillers from Red Fox

GOING TO EGYPT Helen Dunmore

When Dad announces they're going on holiday to Weston, Colette is disappointed – she'd much rather be going to Egypt. But when she meets the boys who ride their horses in the sea at dawn, she realizes that it isn't where you go that counts, it's who you meet while you're there . . .
ISBN 0 09 910901 8 £3.50

BLOOD Alan Durant

Life turns frighteningly upside down when Robert hears his parents have been shot dead in the family home. The police, the psychiatrists, the questions . . . Robert decides to carry out his own investigations, and pushes his sanity to the brink.
ISBN 0 09 992330 0 £3.50

DEL-DEL Victor Kelleher

Des, Hannah and their children are a close-knit family – or so it seems. But suddenly, a year after the death of their daughter Laura, Sam the youngest son starts to act very strangely – having been possessed by a terrifyingly evil presence called Del-Del.
ISBN 0 09 918271 8 £3.50

THE GRANITE BEAST Ann Coburn

After her father's death, Ruth is uprooted from town-life to a close-knit Cornish village and feels lost and alone. But the strange and terrifying dreams she has every night are surely from something more than just unhappiness? Only Ben, another outsider, seems to understand the omen of major disaster . . .
ISBN 0 09 985970 X £2.99

Other great reads from ***Red Fox***

Share the magic of The Magician's House by William Corlett

There is magic in the air from the first moment the three Constant children, William, Mary and Alice arrive at their uncle's house in the Golden Valley. But it's when they meet the Magician, William Tyler, and hear of the Great Task he has for them that the adventures really begin.

THE STEPS UP THE CHIMNEY

Evil threatens Golden House in its hour of need – and the Magician's animals come to the children's aid – but travelling with a fox brings its own dangers.

ISBN 0 09 985370 1   £2.99

THE DOOR IN THE TREE

William, Mary and Alice find a cruel and vicious sport threatening the peace of Golden Valley on their return to this magical place.

ISBN 0 09 997390 1   £2.99

THE TUNNEL BEHIND THE WATERFALL

Evil creatures mass against the children as they attempt to master time travel.

ISBN 0 09 997910 1   £2.99

THE BRIDGE IN THE CLOUDS

With the Magician seriously ill, it's up to the three children to complete the Great Task alone.

ISBN 0 09 918301 9   £2.99